Trust in Molly

By Helen Haraldsen

Trusting Molly

Editing, cover design, and formatting by Let's Get Booked:

www.letsgetbooked.com

Paperback ISBN: 978-1-9160112-7-4

eBook ISBN: 978-1-9160112-8-1

Trusting Molly

BOOK 3

For my husband, Martyn, for all your support.
It means the world.

Contents

- One -

The Gate

Amber Anderson lay on the cold, hard ground, listening to the sound of receding hoof beats galloping away. The darkening sky pushed down on her while the damp ground beneath her pushed back, opposing forces squeezing the air from her lungs.

Gasping for breath, she tried to sit up, but a shooting pain stopped her. Flat on her back, she fumbled for her jacket pocket to find her mobile phone, but where was the zip? She couldn't lift her head to look, so she slowly and painfully removed her gloves and tried again, feeling her way.

At last, Amber found the zip, but dismayed, she discovered the pocket was already open. She must've forgotten to pull the zip up and close the pocket when she set off for the ride. Not so long ago, when she'd needed to help two riders involved in a terrible accident, she'd left her phone in the car. And now, here she was, having made sure she brought it with her while riding out alone, only to have left the pocket open and lost the phone in the fall.

She tilted her head carefully and looked around her. Craning her neck as far as she could bear, Amber spied her phone lying in the mud near the forestry gate. It was way out of her reach.

She couldn't move. *What am I going to do?* Moisture from the damp ground underneath her seeped through her jodhpurs. She couldn't stay there. It was going to be dark soon. Amber tried to turn over onto her side, but again the raw pain stilled her.

I've broken my back, shot into her mind and she gasped.

***

It was October and Amber and her dad had come to the stables straight from school. The hardy Fell ponies were turned out, but Molly spent most of her time living inside. Much to everyone's surprise, she seemed to prefer being stabled. She'd had a few months of being turned out and not ridden over the summer, to see if a rest would help

10

her when she'd been reluctant to jump after the Andersons bought her in the spring. They'd thought some rest and relaxation in the field, enjoying the sunshine and plentiful grass might help her to recover from any little niggly injury the pony might have had, and would also be appreciated after years of being permanently stabled. It hadn't gone quite to plan, however, as Molly had spent most of her time hanging around the field gate as if she wanted to come in. She didn't seem to want to have anything to do with Honey and Pearl – the Fell ponies – and appeared to be more stressed in the field than she was in the stable.

Because she was stabled next to Caroline's horse, Oriel, it was suggested that they try turning Molly out with her instead. This had been a terrible idea. The Andersons had come to the farm one Saturday morning to discover the farmer's daughter in a complete panic. Molly and Oriel had gone missing from the small paddock behind the farmhouse. At first, she'd thought they may have been stolen in the night and was ready to ring the police to report it, but then they'd received a phone call from the police to say that a chestnut pony had been caught running along the bypass several miles away. It was Molly.

The Andersons had rushed off with their trailer to bring the pony home. Thankfully, she was completely unhurt and hadn't caused any accidents on the busy road. It was a miracle really and they were extremely relieved.

But there was no sign of Oriel.

The Blakelys and the Andersons, plus many of their friends and local villagers, searched the surrounding area for hours. Dusk was falling when they finally heard the news that Oricl had been found. Everyone was delighted...until they saw the horse. Oriel had been found underneath a bridge. Whether she had jumped over it or fallen, it wasn't clear, but she was a mess; covered in mud, both of her knees skinned and bloody, but worst of all was her face. Caroline had turned as white as a sheet and cried when she saw the broken bone protruding out of her horse's face like a giant white splinter.

Now, months later, Oriel's knees had healed, although the scars were visible if you looked closely. But her face was forever changed, with a long, ugly bump stretching between her muzzle and forehead.

No-one ever discovered how the horses had got out of the field, but there was an unspoken feeling that the escape was down to Molly, and Oriel had probably followed.

Since then, it was decided that for her own safety, Molly would spend most of her time being stabled. That meant that she needed to be ridden daily, so Mrs Anderson had started hacking her out. She'd never repeated anything like the incident where she bolted with Amber soon after coming to live at Shaw Farm, so that was put down to excitability at hacking off-road for the first time.

***

Now that the winter was approaching, and days were getting shorter, either Mrs Anderson rode Molly during the day if she wasn't at work, or Amber rode her quickly after school.

That day, as she mounted Molly in the yard, her dad asked her, as he always did, which route she was taking while he stayed behind and mucked out Molly's stable.

"I think I'll just go round the roads for half an hour tonight," Amber replied, patting her coat pocket to make sure she had her phone.

Her dad frowned. "With it getting darker now, I think you'd be better sticking to the forestry, away from any traffic."

Looking down on him, Amber frowned back, "but there's hardly any traffic on the roads here. It'll be fine."

"I know, but since we've forgotten to bring your fluorescent, I'd be happier if you weren't on the roads. Go into the forestry, it's safer. And make sure you've got your phone with you."

"Yep, I've got it." She huffed, patting her pocket again, reassured to feel that it was definitely there.

Sighing, Amber rode out of the yard, thinking about her day at school. It had been a non-uniform day. Last year, non-uniform day had been a disaster. Excited at having a day free from the school's bottle green and grey attire, Amber had chosen an outfit that seemed like a good idea at the time: a brown crushed velvet skirt and white blouse. But when she arrived at school, she knew immediately she'd got it wrong. No-one said anything to her, but she could feel the eyes following her and sense the smirks behind her back. She had thought that people would want to use a non-uniform day to look their best and wear nice clothes, but everyone else seemed to know that the new uniform for the day was ripped jeans, T-shirts and hoodies.

So, when the day came around this year, Amber took care to choose something that would help her to blend in instead of stick out and wore black skinny jeans and ballerina pumps with a pale grey slouchy sweater. It had been a huge relief to find that no-one had noticed her all day.

As her daydream reached an end, she arrived at the gate into the forestry. It was normally open, held back with a rock so that riders could go straight through, but today it was closed. Frowning, Amber positioned Molly so that she could reach down to try and open the catch. The Fell ponies would have stood quite happily and let her do this, but Molly had never encountered a closed gate on a ride before and did not understand what she was being asked to do. She was being ridden towards it, but she could not go through it. Confused, she backed up, swung her quarters away and refused to stand still. There was no way Amber could remain mounted and get the gate open.

Mistaking Molly's anxiety for awkwardness, Amber flung herself out of the saddle and dragged the pony impatiently towards the gate. She wrestled with the stiff catch but found it rusty from lack of use, so it was unlikely she could have opened it from Molly's back anyway. Remorse for her irritability nudged heat into her cheeks as, eventually, she was able to release the catch and heave the gate back towards the hedgerow. She pushed the large rock in front of it so that it would still be open when she returned, led Molly through into the forestry and went to remount.

No sooner had she placed her left foot in the stirrup and went to pull herself up into the saddle, than Molly abruptly spun around and charged back through the gate. Amber clung to Molly's left side. Her back smashed into the gatepost as Molly hurtled through the narrow space, sending a sharp pain shooting through her body. The agony threatened to engulf her, but Amber knew that she had to hang on. If she didn't, she would hit the ground hard. And, rider-less, Molly would be heading out back towards the road in the failing light at a flat out gallop. Amber couldn't let that happen.

Grimacing, she dragged herself onto Molly's back, but it was a moving target and she didn't land squarely on the saddle.   Molly's speed and motion bumped her straight off.

Amber barely registered the sickening feeling of falling before she slammed hard onto the ground beneath her.

- Two -

If Only

Molly was gone. Amber was all alone. She couldn't reach her phone to call for help and she couldn't move. There was nothing she could do but look at the sky above her and try not to concentrate on her discomfort and helplessness.

It would be dark soon. Tears leaked from the corners of her eyes as Amber wondered how long it would be before her dad came looking for her. At least he knew where she was. But what about Molly? The pony was loose on the road. Again. Could she be lucky enough to escape unharmed twice? Amber concentrated on her breathing and tried to quell the rising panic that was growing inside her.

It seemed like hours had passed as she lay on the ground – cold, hurt and alone – before car headlights came bobbing up the pot-holed track. With the beam of the lights blinding her as the car came to a stop, her dad jumped out of the driver's seat and ran to her.

Mr Anderson's face was a map of worry as he crouched beside his daughter. The fact that she had lain there on the cold, wet track without getting up meant something was wrong. Could he risk trying to get her in the car or should he phone for an ambulance? They were in the middle of nowhere. It would be hard to try and explain their location to an operator. It could take ages for them to be found, and all the while Amber would be getting colder. It would soon be pitch black too.

Amber was so relieved to have been found, she let out a mighty sob. The force of it jarred her body and sent a wave of torture through her once more. The cocktail of pain and relief combined rushed to her brain in a dizzying assault. But everything would be alright now that her dad was with her.

"It's okay, I'm here, I'm here, shhhhh." Mr Anderson put his arms around her as best as he could. "Do you think you can sit up?" he asked, wrestling with his instinct to keep her still.

"I've tried," Amber gasped, "but I can't. Maybe you could push me up?"

Still terrified of what injuries she may have sustained, but keeping his fears to himself, he slowly and carefully slid his hands under her shoulder blades and began to inch her into a sitting position. Amber winced and gasped. The pain was blinding, and she tasted vomit in her mouth. Everything spun around her like she had just stepped off a fairground ride and the car headlights continued to bore into her like an unrelenting laser. She took a moment to ease the nausea, taking deep breaths of rapidly cooling autumn air, then with her dad's arms still around her, she managed to roll to the left and onto her knees.

"Okay, well done," Mr Anderson's held breath escaped from him like an air brake. "Now I'll try and get you up. Ready?" Amber nodded. Her dad moved to stand in front of her, slotted his arms under her armpits, and began to gently lift. Amber howled with the flash of intense pain that came immediately from her right side.

"Not the right," she managed to hiss out between clenched teeth.

Mr Anderson repositioned himself on her left side and managed to get her to her feet. The ground beneath her lurched away and Mr Anderson had to practically carry her to the passenger side of the car, where he strapped her in without removing her riding hat or gloves. He then rushed to the driver's seat and reversed all the way back down the track. It only took a couple of minutes, but it felt like hours to Amber as every bump and jolt sent sickening waves of agony through her body.

Soon they were onto the main road and heading for the hospital's A & E, which seemed as if it was the place to be on a Friday evening as it was full of people waiting to be seen. Her mother soon arrived to join them and calmly helped her change into a pair of cosy tracky bottoms in a nearby toilet cubicle. Amber winced as her tight, wet jodhs gripped her legs and refused to slide off, meaning Mrs Anderson had to tug at them. She was as gentle as possible but each pull jarred Amber.

Screwing her face up against the pain, she snapped "be...*careful*."

Surprised by the sharpness in her daughter's tone, Mrs Anderson looked up and wondered whether to scold Amber for her curtness. Deciding against it, she replied, "I am, but I can't get them off unless I pull them I'm afraid." Amber made no further protest as her mother continued to coax the jodhpurs off her until they sat in a defeated soggy pile on the cubicle floor. She was helped into her tracky bottoms and they returned to the waiting room in silence.

While they waited to be called, Amber heard snatches of the conversation between her parents as she concentrated on blocking out the discomfort. The large pink pill given to her by a triage nurse upon her arrival hadn't helped much with the pain.

"...just wheeling the barrow out...Molly flying back into the yard...no Amber!"

"...did you do?"

"...house...only Caroline in...she offered... straight in the car... my fault... I told her to...gate closed... if only..."

At least Molly is alright, Amber thought to herself. It sounded as if Caroline had looked after the pony so that her dad could come to find her straight away. She wanted

22

to tell her dad that it wasn't his fault; he seemed to be blaming himself for telling her to go into the forestry, instead of on the roads as she'd planned, but a weariness had come over her, out of nowhere, and she just slumped against him, the words unspoken.

She must've fallen asleep somehow, for when she awoke, Amber was being wheeled up a squeaky linoleum corridor towards the X-ray department in a hard, uncomfortable wheelchair.

It turned out that she had broken her right collarbone. The doctor showed them a picture of the X-ray and Amber could see the bone was clearly in two halves.

"Not to worry," the doctor said, clipping a pen back into the breast pocket of his white jacket. "Although a broken collarbone can be extremely painful, it should heal well in around six weeks. You must keep it supported at all times with a simple sling and try to avoid moving your arm. If it swells up, use an ice pack, and normal painkillers should be enough to make the discomfort bearable."

Great, thought Amber. *Six weeks? That means no riding for six whole weeks.*

And as well as the riding, there was something else she wasn't going to be able to do now too. Her friend Joanne was *not* going to be happy.

- Three -

A Change of Plan

"You've done *what?*" cried Joanne when she opened her door to see Amber standing with her arm in a sling and an explanation at the ready.

***

When she'd come home from the hospital the previous evening, she'd planned on sending a WhatsApp message to her best friends, Joanne and Emily, to explain what had happened, but by the time she'd struggled out of her clothes and into a bath – it was very hard to get into a bath with only one working arm, she'd discovered – and then into pyjamas and bed, she'd been so exhausted she'd fallen asleep immediately. This morning had been another struggle to do everything without disturbing her arm. Eventually, much later than usual on a Saturday morning, the Andersons were ready to drive to the yard. Although Amber wouldn't be riding for a while, the ponies still needed seeing to and Molly needed to be exercised.

Her dad crawled up the farm track, taking even greater care than usual to avoid the potholes. When they reached Jubilee House, where her friend Joanne lived, Amber asked to be dropped off at the door. She couldn't help with mucking out or be any use at the yard, so she figured she might as well break the news to Jo and get it over with.

"You should go for a ride," she told her parents as she clambered laboriously out of the back seat, "I'll just hang around here for a while."

"You can't invite yourself to stay here for hours," her mother tutted, "they may be busy or going out or something. I'll come and ask Lou if it's okay."

"Oh, you needn't do that," Amber moaned grumpily as her mother went to undo her seatbelt, "I'll find out if it's okay for me to stay and I'll text you if there's any problem."

"Well...alright then," her mother conceded. "But make sure you ask politely."

Amber pulled a sarcastic face. These last couple of months, since she'd started back at school in Year 8 and her 13th birthday approached, she'd found herself getting a bit moody. Although her parents sometimes bore the brunt of her recent mood swings, she always knew to be well-mannered with everyone else.

When the door of Jubilee House opened, it wasn't Lou Jones, Joanne's mum who opened the door, but Joanne herself. Her eyes turned to saucers when she saw Amber and her frown was a question she didn't need to ask out loud.

"I came off Molly last night. Broke my collarbone." She tried to shrug apologetically, forgetting momentarily that she hadn't to move. She grimaced.

"You've done *what?*"

Amber arranged her face into what she hoped resembled a rueful expression. It wasn't like she had done this on purpose, but it was going to ruin Jo's plans.

"How're you going to do the postal shoot now?"

***

Since Amber had discovered that her parents' meek, mild Fell pony, Honey, was a surprise cross-country star at Pony Club camp that summer, she'd spent the rest of the season competing her. Molly, her competition pony, had been side-lined with a suspected injury and given the summer off, so when Honey proved herself to be unexpectedly keen on jumping, she had been taken to all the local Pony Club gymkhanas and autumn hunter trials, and had even gone as far as Hexham for the Fell Pony Performance Trials.

Honey loved to jump, but she wasn't very fast, and however fit she got, her stamina wasn't the best. Amber was amassing quite a collection of green and orange rosettes – the colours given for fourth and fifth place. So, it was a huge shock when they managed to win the junior section of Brantfort Pony Club's hunter trial last month. Honey always went clear everywhere she went, but lost out on the time penalties she picked up. However, there was something about the ditch on this course that was catching even experienced horses and ponies out. Not Honey though; she popped over it in her usual cheerful fashion. Then, near the end was the water jump, sited in a

28

boggy area of the field. The water did look pretty gross – it was brown and murky with green algae snaking across the surface – and lots of riders had to take the alternative to avoid being eliminated at it, as so many ponies refused to enter the swamp. Honey didn't care. Perhaps because she'd spent her early years living wild on the fells of Caldbeck, a bit of bog was nothing out of the ordinary for her and she splashed through the gunge without a care in the world. She still came back with her customary time faults that day…but she was the only clear round. Nobody could believe that a Fell pony who had been a riding school pony all her life could go out and beat combinations who regularly competed at affiliated level.

Amber's confidence had skyrocketed and Honey became a local celebrity. It seemed like everyone knew her, and even when they went, as their last competition of the season, to the Fell Pony Performance Trials, they found that people there, whom they'd never met, had heard of her too.

Meanwhile, Joanne, who had recovered from a terrible accident just over a year ago, and had been schooling up a new pony, had also begun to compete again. Her pale palomino, Merry, despite being rather careless at show jumping, was a cross-country machine, going fast and clear at every event. This had given Jo an idea that she had put to Amber during a sleepover at Jubilee House a couple of weeks ago.

"A what? A...trackalon?" Amber said when she'd heard the strange term Jo had used.

"No...I've told you before - tetrathlon," Jo had laughed at Amber's mispronunciation. "It's a Pony Club competition that involves riding cross-country, which both our ponies are brilliant at."

"Yes, but what else? You said there were four phases."

"Yeah, there are. You also have to shoot, run and swim. The order is usually shoot first, then swim, then ride and run last."

"Whoa...hang on. Shoot? What do you mean shoot? Shoot what... and with what?"

"At a target with an air pistol," Jo replied casually.

"What? They let children use guns?" Amber couldn't believe what she was hearing.

"Yes, but for minimus and juniors, an adult has to load the gun. Everything is perfectly safe."

"Yeah, but there's one small problem." Amber pointed out. "Where are we going to get a gun from?"

"Oh, we've already got one. Brantfort Pony Club are going to run a tetrathlon for local branches next summer. They used to do it apparently, but haven't for ages. Now they've got a new DC, she's keen to get it going again. When I told my parents I wanted to do it, they were well up for it and my dad found out about postal shoots that run through the winter to let competitors practise their shooting. So he's going to run it for our branch and he bought a gun for me and Matthew to share. You could borrow it too and join in. Then you'll be ready to compete next summer."

Amber went to speak but Joanne, clearly excited with her plan, ploughed on and cut her off.

"And, if we can get two other girls to do it, we could be a team and aim for the Area Qualifier!"

***

A team hadn't yet been sorted out, but the postal shoot was imminent, with the first round due to start in less than a fortnight, during the October half-term. Amber was meant to have been using the time now, before it began, to practise with the gun and get used to it so that

31

her performance in the competition would be helped. But now there was one obvious, major complication: Amber was right-handed…and now she couldn't even move her right arm, let alone grip a gun, lift her arm, hold it steady to aim, and fire.

"I don't think I can," she replied to Jo's question. "Unless I can shoot left-handed!" she added as a joke.

But Jo's head snapped up and she looked fiercely at Amber, determination hardening her pretty face.

"Come with me." She reached forward and took hold of Amber's uninjured left arm, pulling her into the house.

"Ow!" Amber cried, as she lurched forward and jolted her shoulder.

"Oh, sorry, sorry!" Jo hurriedly let go of Amber and closed the door behind her. "But I have a plan. DAAAAAAAAAAAAAAAAAAAAAAD!"

- *Four* -

Shoot!

When Amber's parents had come to pick her up to go home after their ride on Molly and Honey, they were chased away by Joanne who had been seized by an ardent fervour and insisted that Amber stayed for a sleepover. Mrs Anderson had fussed for a bit about Amber's arm and her sling and not having a change of clothes or a toothbrush, but Jo had dismissed these concerns, insisting that she would lend Amber whatever she needed and would help her to get dressed. Mrs Jones had been happy for Amber to stay and so she, Jo and Matthew were now standing in Jo's garage. Amber held a gun in her left hand.

***

Mr Jones had been summoned, following Amber's throwaway comment about shooting left-handed, to see if it would be possible.

The garage had been set up with a bench in the middle, set seven metres away from a row of targets at the far end which were pinned to an old mattress.

"It's to stop the bullets ricocheting back and hitting you," declared Matthew, who was the most animated Amber had ever seen him. "That's what would happen if the targets were against a hard surface."

Amber looked questioningly at Jo and her dad to see if this was true or if Matthew was pulling her leg.

"Yes, it could happen," Mr Jones confirmed, "but 'bullets' is a bit of an exaggeration. They're just pellets, and the pistols are low power so they wouldn't do you much harm. But obviously, there are a lot of safety rules to prevent anyone from being accidentally shot."

Amber watched with interest as Jo and Matthew each took turns to shoot at a target with their gun. Mr Jones loaded the gun for them after each shot; Amber noted that it only held one pellet at a time, and even though it was only an informal practice, he gave commands like 'are you ready?', 'standby' and 'reload' to prepare them for what it would be like in a tetrathlon competition.

Matthew was delighted to be eligible to take part as competitors had to be at least nine-years-old to be allowed to shoot. Although his tenth birthday was coming up in December, he would still be competing in the minimus class next summer. As such, he was allowed to stand square on to the target and hold the gun with both hands, but Jo and herself would compete as juniors which meant they were only allowed to use one hand. Jo was either very well-practised or very strong as Amber noticed that her arm didn't tremble at all when she raised the gun, aimed quickly and fired within the four-second count down provided by Mr Jones.

"In the tetrathlon, juniors have a turning target, which means that when it turns to face you, you've only got four seconds to aim and shoot before it turns away again," Jo explained, "which is why you have to get used to the time allowed. We don't have turning targets here, so for the postal shoot, we'll just be using a static target like the minimus, but you've still only got four seconds to make the shot."

Amber nodded gently, remembering not to make any movement that would jolt her arm. There was a lot to take in.

"Okay then, Amber," Mr Jones pointed to where she should stand, behind the bench. "As you're right-handed, you'd normally stand with your right shoulder towards the target. You'd hold the gun in your right hand, close your left eye and look through the sights with your right, aiming for the bull's eye in the middle, then gently squeeze the trigger. But as your right arm is going to be out of play for a while, you're going to have to at least start the postal shoot using your left. You'll be able to swap back to your right when you're all healed, which will be in plenty of time for the tetrathlon next summer."

Amber stood where she was directed and turned her left shoulder towards the target as Mr Jones handed her the unloaded gun. She curled her fingers around the handgrip and lifted it tentatively. Mr Jones showed her how to raise the gun and line up the centre of the target with the front and rear sights of the pistol. She practised a few times but found her arm shaking at the weight of the gun. Mr Jones noticed and sent Jo into the house to bring some drinks and biscuits while Amber had a rest.

After a snack of crumbly Hobnobs and some sweet apple juice, it was time for Amber to try a real target. When she saw Mr Jones open the top of the pistol, push the pellet into it and snap it closed, she blinked rapidly and took a deep, steadying breath. She wished that Jo and Matthew hadn't stayed to watch her first attempt – they were both so good. Their targets had been full of neat little holes in the bull's eye, worth ten points, and the next band of eight points. Jo's target had been particularly precise, with a cluster of holes in and around the bull's eye. Amber had a strong suspicion that she would not be a good shot. Her hand-eye coordination wasn't the best and she couldn't catch anything smaller than a netball. She always dreaded any PE at school that involved catching or hitting balls: tennis, rounders, hockey, as she was so bad at them. It didn't help either that her eyesight wasn't brilliant, and it was about time she got herself some glasses. It was going to be a repeat of her first attempt at jumping with Pearl, when Jo and Matthew cleared the fences effortlessly on their ponies while Pearl had embarrassed her by being ridiculously stubborn and refusing tiny cross poles. This was going to be another of those episodes. She just knew it.

"Are you ready?" This was her signal to pick up the gun.

"Standby."

"Fire."

As Mr Jones began to count, Amber raised the gun hurriedly, attempted to line up the sights and pulled the trigger just as "three" was being said.

"Four…stop." Mr Jones finished.

Amber placed the gun back on the bench as Mr Jones looked at the target through his binoculars. "I'm afraid that shot is off-target," he relayed as he scanned the unmarked target ahead of him. "You panicked and rushed. There was still plenty of time. Let's do a few more."

Amber took four more shots, trying hard to block out everything except the gun sights in front of her and the distant target. When she managed to get her fourth and fifth shots into the four and six point bands, Jo whooped and clapped behind her. Feeling slightly more encouraged, she took another rest, this time with some lemonade and a giant bag of marshmallows that Matthew produced with a smirk. Nothing was said, but Amber was sure they weren't his to share.

Of Amber's final five shots, three were on target: two fours and a two. She was disappointed that only half of her ten shots found the target at all, and none were anywhere near the bullseye. But her left arm was trembling and there was an ache developing across her chest as her collarbone throbbed. Even though she'd used her left arm, it felt as if her injured side had also been involved, and it wasn't pleased. It grumbled indignantly, as if reminding Amber that she was supposed to be resting it.

Despite her despondency at her poor performance, Jo was delighted and congratulated Amber at her first attempt.

"That was amazing," she enthused. "I can't do anything with my left hand at all. I'd never have been able to hit the target in a million years with my left. You're so clever!"

Amber blushed at her praise, which she didn't feel was deserved, but it was so like Jo to be encouraging.

Jo was all for Amber continuing and trying some more shots, but when Amber explained that she was starting to feel uncomfortable, she was whisked up to Jo's room and made to lie on her bed with a hot chocolate, topped with some more of the marshmallows.

Amber sighed with contentment as she lay in the comfort of the bedcovers, looking at the horse and pony posters that decorated the walls and the bookshelves filled with Jo's pony books, toys, ornaments, rosettes and framed pictures of her jumping her old pony, Flash, at various competitions.

Just as she wondered wearily what might be for tea and what plans her friend might have in store for them that evening, Jo appeared in the room. She sat on the bed beside Amber and removed the empty mug she was still holding in her left hand, swapping it for something blue and squishy.

"What's this?" Amber asked in surprise, looking down to see a blue-haired ball with two eyes peering up at her.

"It's a stress ball. Mum and the other teachers were given one at work. It's for you to squeeze to build up the muscles in your left hand to improve your grip on the gun. Go on, give him a squeeze."

Amber clenched her palm. It was harder than it looked.

"Harder!" commanded Jo, her face looking at the blue ball keenly.

Amber gave the ball another squeeze, surprised at how little power she had in her left hand. Jo's expectant gaze was replaced with a look of chagrin. She reached out and took the ball from Amber, and with her right hand, squeezed it hard. Amber laughed as the two eyes attached to the ball shot out on stalks, which, combined with the pointy blue hair, gave it a highly startled appearance.

"This is what you're aiming for," Jo instructed. "You've got to get your left hand strong enough to make his eyes pop right out. That's your homework from now on, right?"

Amber could tell from Jo's stern expression that she meant it, so she nodded and took the ball back, giving it the hardest squeeze she could manage. The eyes wobbled slightly but did not leap out.

"Right, athlete in training here. You need building up. Let's go and see what's for tea."

- Five -

Pink

Two weeks later, it was half term. The first Friday evening saw Amber at Mrs Best's house for a stable management rally. Amber had taken and passed her D and D+ tests that summer and was now working towards her C test. This meant that she was still in group 2, which was annoying as her friend Emily had moved into group 1 as she was now aiming for her C+. Emily went to the same school as Amber but as she was in Year 9 – the year above – she hardly got to see her. Although Joanne was now back to full health after her accident, and would be in Amber's group, as she too was aiming for her C test, Amber was desperate to see Emily and speak to her properly. Emily had been a godsend to her earlier in the year at her first Pony Club camp and she'd been delighted for her friend when she'd won the final One Day Event competition at the end of the week, beating their nemesis – the nasty Elisha Templeton. Amber hadn't understood why Emily had seemed so sad at the end of the week when she should have been on cloud nine, but later on, over the summer holidays, she'd found out a bit more.

Emily hadn't been to many competitions over the summer but they'd kept in touch through messages. Amber had learned at camp, through a vicious outburst from Elisha, that Emily's dad had lost his job as the company he worked for as a kitchen fitter had closed down. He'd managed to get a bit of freelance work, but no permanent job. With money uncertain and winter approaching, Emily had been told that her beloved pony, Fudge, might have to be sold. Emily was understandably heart-broken as her 'Freaky Treacle' was the love of her life. On the few occasions when Amber had seen Emily around school before the summer holidays, and since their return in September, she could tell the girl wasn't herself. Instead of being surrounded by a gang of friends, all giggling and relaxed as usual, Emily had looked tired and was more withdrawn from her friends.

But today, at lunchtime, Emily had run up behind Amber and poked her in the ribs, making Amber squeal in shock. When she whipped round to see who her assailant was, Emily's twinkling hazel eyes looked back at her and she registered her friend's huge grin.

"My dad's got a job!" she said, bouncing with excitement. "Oh, bountiful providence!" Emily did a twirl, then closed her hands together in prayer and aimed them at the ceiling as if she was thanking God for this change in circumstances. Amber was pleased to see her return to her usual playful self.

"That's brilliant. So, does that mean you can keep Fudgey?"

"Yes. Fudge is staying, and there's more. I've got a surprise for you." Emily looked as if she could barely contain herself. She was like a fizzy drink that had been shaken and then opened. Emily's bubbling happiness was infectious.

"What is it? What's the surprise?" Amber squeaked in a girly voice, most unlike her.

But just then the end-of-lunch bell clamoured and people started jostling to get to their lessons. Emily was swept up in a wave of moving bodies and carried away like a boat on the tide.

"Fizzlesticks. I'll tell you tonight at the rally," she called, still beaming as she was sucked into the surge of green uniforms and disappeared.

Amber had to endure the rest of the day at school wondering what her news could be, and when she arrived at the rally, desperate to speak to her, she didn't get the chance as Emily was quickly sent outside to join her group who were in the stables looking at first aid and learning how to apply a poultice to a horse's leg. Amber's group had also been scheduled to look at some basic first aid and how to deal with minor wounds, but since Amber could not participate, with her arm still in a sling, they were staying in the house to watch videos and discuss signs of ill health in a pony.

Sitting with Jo and Matthew, who was now aiming for his D and D+ tests, Amber noted the others in their group: Jake, who had been in her group at camp in the summer and a new boy with a happy, friendly face that looked somehow familiar.

Eventually, the videos of ponies with snotty noses, runny eyes, sweet itch and mild colic ended and Amber was finally able to get outside and speak with Emily while they waited for their parents to stop eating the cakes and other goodies provided by Mrs Best. The sweet treats ensured parents brought their children to Friday night stable management rallies, instead of conking out on the sofa in front of Coronation Street.

"Soooo." She grabbed her friend's arm and pulled her away from the rest of the group as Emily left the stable of the horse they'd all been poulticing. "What's your big news then?"

Emily plunged her hand into her hoody pocket and pulled out her phone. A few swipes later, she was holding it out towards Amber and Joanne, who had come out with Amber to hear Emily's news too.

"Boom, shake the room. Meet my new pony!"

Amber swiftly took the phone and held it up for a closer inspection. She nearly bumped heads with Jo as she also crowded in to see the screen. The picture they saw showed a beaming Emily mounted on a spectacular pink pony. Amber knew from her horse books that the colour was strawberry roan: bay with white hairs mixed in to

46

produce what looked like a pink coat. The pony had black legs and a black tail. But the pony's head and neck were what really grabbed Amber's attention. There was a perfectly formed white diamond right in the centre of its forehead and the mane was hogged but growing out so that it resembled a black Mohican. Amber had never seen a more striking pony in all her life.

"This is Pink, AKA Sunset Friday," Emily said, looking over their shoulders at the picture.

"Wha…?" Amber was speechless. A new pony? It had looked like there was going to be no pony and now there were two.

"My dad is now a fitness instructor at the new gym in town and he loves it. He's so happy he's agreed to let me have a new pony as I'm growing out of Fudge. I went to try her last weekend and she's being delivered tomorrow. I can't wait! She's got a good competition record, but she's been a bit of a naughty minx with her current rider. That's how come we can afford her. But I'm sure we'll be a totally amazing team in no time." Emily explained.

"Wow, that's amazing, and not what I was expecting at all." Amber handed the phone back after taking one final look at the pony in the picture, and hugged Emily. She could feel her friend's excitement rippling through her like a mini-earthquake. "I'm so happy for you…but what about Fudge?"

"He's been so good to me, my little angel. He's looked after me for years and taught me everything I know. But it's time for him to teach someone new."

"But…I…I thought you said Fudge was staying?

"He is. Don't worry, I'll never part with my boy and now he's getting a girlfriend to keep him company." The girls turned to face the house just as a man and boy came out of the door and walked towards them.

"Fudge is going to be showing my little brother the ropes."

Then it dawned on Amber. The new boy in her group with the big smile and friendly eyes had seemed familiar because he looked just like Emily. He was her little brother!

"Amber, Jo, meet Harry. And this is my dad."

"Hi," the little boy said, without a hint of shyness.

"Hi," both girls said in unison, smiling back at him. Amber surreptitiously took in Emily's dad, whom she had never seen before. He looked quite intimidating and not like his children at all, who both resembled their mother. He wasn't terribly tall but he had a shaved head, and although he was wearing a baggy sweatshirt and jeans, Amber could tell from the width of his neck and shoulders that he was made of muscle.

"Er…hello, Mr Pryde," she said, her voice faltering slightly.

"Oh, call me Phil," he said, his eyes smiling in the same way that Emily and Harry's did. They lit up his face and suddenly softened his rather fierce first impression.

"Can't wait to see Pink," she told Emily as they parted. "Make sure you put loads of photos and videos on Instagram.

"Course. You'll be sick of the sight of her before Christmas."

As Emily's car pulled out of the yard and they stood shivering as they waited for Amber's dad and Jo's mum to come out of the house with Matthew, Jo turned to Amber. "I wonder if Emily's new pony has done much cross-country?" she wondered aloud.

Amber read her mind. "You're thinking she could be a tetrathlon team member."

"I am. You can compete with a team of three, but it means everyone's score has to count then. It's best if you can have four on a team, then if anyone has a disaster, their score can be dropped as only the best three count."

"So, we just need one more person, as well as Emily."

"Yes, and I think I know who it should be."

- Six -

Jo Takes Charge

Half term flew by and it was soon time to go back to school. Amber had thought she'd be bored stiff with no riding to do over the week off, but she'd gone with her parents to the farm and spent most of her week off with Jo. Mrs Jones hadn't minded as she was a teacher so had the week off too.

Sometimes, she'd sat on an oil drum and watched Jo school Merry over the show jumps or hand-made cross-country fences in their own fields, sometimes they went in the garage and practised aiming the unloaded pistol at targets. Mr Jones was at work and they weren't allowed to shoot the gun without him there. A few times, Amber had managed to cling, one-handed, onto the back of Jo on her bike as she and Matthew rode up to the forestry to build a camp among the trees. Her arm didn't hurt her as much now, though when Jo hit a couple of potholes as she rode up the track, it sent a lightning bolt of agony through her that made her eyes water. She didn't complain and Jo was none the wiser, since Amber was behind her where she couldn't see.

Building a camp had been exciting and she'd done what she could to carry slender branches and moss to the site of a fallen pine tree. They'd used its upturned roots and the mud and stones still attached to them as one wall and then constructed two more using debris they'd found on the forest floor. Because the camp was made entirely from natural resources, and was well away from the forestry tracks, it was impressively camouflaged. But the three of them found it easily every time they returned. They had named it Pine Cone Cottage but the week had run out before they'd had a chance to make a door and a roof. It would have to wait.

During her time spent with Jo, she learned of her plan for the tetrathlon team that did not yet exist but which Jo was already enthusiastically managing.

"So, I thought we could ask Chelsea Connor to be the fourth member," she said one day, while they were in the garage pretending to shoot with the pistol.

Amber knew of Chelsea from camp. She rode a grey mare named Skylark and had come second to Emily in the end-of-camp One Day Event after the pony had initially refused to jump the gate into the dark wooded section of the course. She'd noted that Chelsea seemed like a pretty gutsy rider during the week as her pony wasn't always easy but she always got what she wanted from it in the end.

"Hmm," Amber considered. "Though isn't her pony more of a showjumper than a cross-country-er? I'd thought, maybe Natalie would be good. She seems to be doing really well with Rocky now."

Amber had met Natalie, a new member, earlier that year at the first mounted rally of the season. Natalie's pony, Sable, had been a complete witch and it was clear she was going to destroy Natalie's confidence as she wasn't an experienced rider. So, it had come as a great shock when Natalie had bought Rocky from Elisha Templeton, a pony Amber considered unpredictable and dangerous following his involvement in the accident that could have killed Joanne and her pony, Flash.

But everyone had watched with amazement over the summer as Natalie and Rocky had struck up an immediate bond and in no time were jumping one-metre show jumping tracks with ease. Rocky seemed to have settled and looked much more relaxed when ridden by Natalie than he had when Elisha had been his rider. Amber was both impressed and a little jealous of their swift progress. She knew all about the dangers of envying others and had learned that lesson with Pearl during their first year together. But she couldn't help sometimes letting that little jealous voice in her mind get a few digs in at her. *See*, it would say to her, *there's Natalie doing brilliantly with her new pony, while your competition pony does nothing 'cos you're scared of her.*

"Shut up," Amber would tell the voice and she'd convince herself that she admired the way Natalie adapted to such a high-powered pony so quickly and easily, while she herself struggled to bond with Molly, the trophy-winning pony her parents had bought for her to compete on.

Jo interrupted her thoughts. "I don't really know Natalie so maybe, but Chelsea would be good, I think. Yes, Skye has done more show jumping as she used to be Chelsea's sister's pony and they did BS together but she's given up riding now and Chelsea has taken her on. I think she's always been a bit in Imogen's shadow and is quite determined to be noticed too. Nothing like a bit of sibling rivalry."

Amber didn't know about Chelsea and her sister so she asked, "Why did her sister give up riding if she was so good at it?"

Jo put the gun on the bench and picked up Amber's squeezy blue ball that she was using to strengthen the grip in her left hand. "Catch," she said tossing it to Amber, who reached out her left hand, but missed, and had to bend down to pick it up from the dusty garage floor. "Skye was Imogen's pony. For some reason, they'd gone to some unaffiliated Pony Club event, which wasn't their usual scene. They did British Showjumping, as I said. At the event, there were a few cross-country fences in the field next to where the show jumping was. There was a separate competition to have a go at the six or seven cross-country fences, and the person who could do it fastest in each age group would be the winner. So, Imogen had a go. She was competitive so she was going for the time, but the last fence was a staircase of three steps to be jumped down. Imogen had lost control of Skye and they were flying as they came to the steps. Skye didn't seem to know what she was meant to do with the three steps so she just jumped them all in one go. Imogen flew right out of the saddle and was badly hurt. But more than that, when she was recovered, she refused to get back on. That was it. She just gave up. She does hockey and netball now, I think. Star captain of the teams."

"So, Chelsea took over the ride on Skye?" Amber asked, squeezing the ball absentmindedly.

"Yes, she was also doing a bit of show jumping too, but was never as successful as Imogen so she'd started to get into gymnastics. I think she'd wanted something where they couldn't be compared to each other all the time. But now Imogen has given up, Chelsea has taken over the ride on Skye, though I think she's more interested in eventing than just show jumping so she's introducing Skye to cross-country. They've been doing quite well I think, and with her background in gymnastics, she's bound to be quite athletic and fit. Perfect for the running and swimming phases."

"So, what are we going to do then?" Amber squeezed the ball in Jo's face. Jo laughed as the white plastic eyes bulged towards her. "There are three potential people for only two places: Emily, Chelsea and Natalie. We can't tell them all and then leave one person out."

"People can compete as individuals too."

"Yes, but it's not nice to think you're going to be on a team and then get left out," Amber pointed out. She suspected Jo had little experience of being left out of sporting teams. She, on the other hand, knew the feeling all too well.

"Yeah, I suppose so. Hmmm, I'll have to think about that one."

While Jo was concentrating, Amber tickled her under the nose with the pointy blue hair of her squeezy ball. "Well don't hurt your brain whatever you do," she teased, boldly.

"Cheeky!"

– Seven –

Team Trainer

As it turned out, Joanne didn't have to worry about who to pick for 'her' team as the matter was taken out of her hands.

Amber's phone buzzed on the Monday evening of the first day back at school. She was lost in reading a book she had to review for English homework. It was one set by the teacher and usually Amber hated reading books she was told to read, instead of ones she could choose herself, but this one was pretty good, despite being a classic, which normally meant difficult and boring in her experience. She ignored her phone until she reached the end of a chapter. When she eventually picked it up, she saw there was a message from Jo.

Have you seen??????? It said, the overuse of question marks implying a sense of urgency.

Seen what? She replied.

The Blakefield Facebook page! There's a post on reminding everyone that the first round of the postal shoot is this weekend and it also asks anyone interested in taking part in Brantfort's branch tetrathlon to message their names to Mrs Best 😲

Okay. What's up with that??

We were going to sort out our own team! Now we won't be able to decide anything as it'll all be run by adults!!!!

Amber wasn't surprised that the club was going to organise everything as it was a Pony Club competition, and couldn't understand why Jo was so upset. She surely couldn't have expected to have been in charge...she was eleven! Amber considered how she could put this tactfully in a message and deleted several attempts before she finally sent off:

Maybe for the best, then the problem of who to pick and who to leave out is for them to worry about not us 😊

Dots appeared showing that Jo was typing a message back but it was several minutes before her reply appeared. Amber guessed she was also struggling to find the right words. In the end, all that came through was a ☹

Instead of going back to her book, Amber opened Instagram and scrolled through various posts to see if Emily had posted anything new. During half term, there had been a daily picture showing what she was getting up to with Pink, but now, with it being term time and the clocks had gone back, there was no possibility of riding after school.

There was nothing new from Emily, but there was a post from Natalie the previous day showing her with Elisha, both holding up rosettes they'd won at an indoor show.

Since her humiliation at camp, when her young event horse had been eliminated on the cross-country course, Elisha had turned her focus away from eventing and back to the world of show jumping. Her horse, Thunder Cat, hadn't been bold with ditches and water fences, but he was a scopey and precise showjumper and she was cleaning up at BS shows around the country. Amber was pleased. Although she couldn't stand Elisha, the fact that she was doing so well at affiliated shows meant that she'd probably stay away from 'poxy' local Pony Club events, which meant that Amber wouldn't have to see her. It was a shame though that Elisha seemed to have adopted Natalie and now took her along with her in her huge horsebox to shows. It looked unlikely that Amber would be seeing much of her either.

Just as she was liking Natalie's post, her phone pinged with a message. It was from Emily. As Amber read it, her left eyebrow arched. This was not good news. Jo would not be happy.

***

The next day at school, Amber forced herself to hang around the Year Nine locker area before the bell went for morning registration, hoping to find Emily. She was nowhere to be seen and Amber found herself receiving some strange looks from the Year Nines, who were clearly wondering why she was there. She returned at break time, much to the delight of her friend Sarah who had wanted an excuse to hang around there to be able to spy on a boy she fancied.

This time Amber was in luck. She stood next to Emily as she opened her locker to put her PE kit in. She was flushed and her hair had frizzed showing she'd had the pleasure of period one PE outside in the drizzle.

"Your dad is going to be coaching the tetrathlon teams?" she asked immediately to confirm that Emily's message last night hadn't been some sort of joke. Emily knew that Amber and Jo were keen to be on a team but she hadn't expressed much interest when the idea of her joining them had been suggested.

"Urgh, yeah," Emily groaned, wrestling with her lumpy kit bag which refused to fit into the narrow locker space.

"Why?" She'd never seen Emily's dad at any events and had assumed he didn't have much interest in her hobby, since his previous job had been Monday to Friday. That meant he wasn't working on Sundays and so *could* have come to watch her.

"Oh, because he's always been a fitness freak, running marathons and going to the gym all weekend…"

Ah, that explains why he never came to any shows then, thought Amber.

"But now he's got this job as a fitness instructor, he's even more obsessed and wants to volunteer his services to Blakefield to help the club." She said this last part sarcastically and Amber wondered what she meant by it. Emily didn't elaborate but Amber could tell she was not at all happy with the news.

"Are you doing it?" she asked, sensing what the answer would be.

With a mighty heave, Emily finally managed to force her kit bag into the locker and slammed the door. She turned around and leant wearily against the cold metal.

"Well, I wouldn't have been. I HATE running and I mean HATE it. I'm just not built for it with my long body and short legs, but Dad told me I have to. "If I'm the trainer, it wouldn't look very good if my own daughter wasn't involved would it?" Emily mimicked her father's voice with absolute accuracy. "So, my life is going to be hell because I'm not like him, I'm not sporty. But he's really competitive so he'll be pushing me – us – all the time, I know it. He's never bothered about my lack of sporting ability before, as he's had Harry and his cricket and football to concentrate on, but now, with this, I'll be like his advert so he'll be determined for me to be great, and I just won't be."

Amber was shocked to see her friend look so stricken. She was teary, which was so unlike her as she was always positive and upbeat. She cast around for something to say but couldn't think of anything useful. *Why do I never know what to say?* Whether she wanted to offer comfort or a cutting retaliation to wound a bully, Amber could never summon the words she needed until around three hours later when it was too late. Saved by the bell ringing, she gave Emily a quick hug, then dragged Sarah away from where she was gawping at a boy with a crop of curls on his head so long and thick it made him resemble one of those mop-top sheep. She couldn't see the attraction herself.

She didn't see Emily around school for the rest of the week and she was busy with lots of homework. She sent Jo a message to tell her the news about Emily's dad being the tetrathlon team trainer and was surprised to get no response from her. She'd expected a series of outraged messages with lots of angry emojis, but she got nothing.

What does that mean? she wondered. *Oh well, I'll see her on Saturday for the first round of the postal shoots. Then I'll find out.*

- Eight -

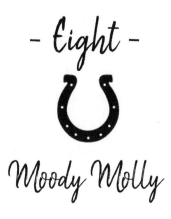

Moody Molly

Amber was sitting on Jo's bed. She'd been dropped off there by her parents before they went on to the farm to see to the ponies. It was the first day of the postal shoot and she'd been expecting to do her first target, but Mr Jones had an idea.

"Everyone has to submit twelve targets – three per month. But rather than do one each week while your right arm is injured, you could just wait another three weeks and do your first three all in one go, once you're healed, rather than having to do it with the handicap of using your left."

She hadn't known what to say as she could see the logic in Mr Jones' suggestion but she was looking forward to shooting her first competitive target. Amber could now squeeze the blue ball hard enough to make his eyes shoot out and she'd even been practising maintaining her grip so that his poppy eyes stayed out on their stalks for as long as possible. She was prepared. It was true, though, that she'd be getting her sling off in a couple of weeks and would be able to use her right hand. Reluctantly, she'd nodded her agreement and gone in the house with Jo to wait for her parents to return and collect her.

"So…you mean you don't want to do it anymore?" asked Amber, incredulously. Jo had just told her that she wasn't bothered about Mr Pryde nominating himself as tetrathlon team trainer, as she wasn't going to be doing any training with him.

"No, I still want to do it," Jo explained, whilst deftly putting her shoulder-length blonde hair into a perfect French plait. "We've put my name forward for the junior girls' team, even though I'm still actually only eleven on the 1st of January, which is when your age is counted from, so, technically I could compete as a minimus. But even if there are more than four junior girls, I'm sure to be picked, as I'm good at all four phases. I live miles away from you and Emily's area though, so I'll just do my own thing. I can already do tumble turns and three minutes of swimming is no problem. The only thing I need to practise is running 1,500 metres, but I can run around our own fields or in the forestry." She quickly secured the end of her plait with a pony's plaiting band and plonked herself on the end of her bed.

"You'll have to teach me how to do that. I can't do a thing with my own hair except put it in a ponytail." She flicked her trademark ponytail to demonstrate.

"Ohh, yeah. You've got such lovely, long, thick hair. It would look great in a French plait."

Jo worked on Amber's hair until a car horn sounded outside and Amber had to rush off. It hadn't taken her parents long as it was a wet day and they'd obviously decided to just do a short ride to let Molly stretch her legs so she wasn't in the stable all day. Not that the pony seemed to mind. Mrs Anderson sometimes joked that Molly was agoraphobic since she never seemed to be pleased to get out of her stable.

As Amber still couldn't lift her right arm, she hadn't been able to try plaiting her own hair, but Jo had shown her how to overlap the strands and Amber climbed into the car sporting a perfect plait.

"How did it go?" her father asked over his shoulder to Amber in the back seat.

"Oh...I didn't shoot today." She explained Mr Jones' idea. Mr Anderson detected the disappointment in his daughter's voice and cast around for an idea to cheer her up.

"I'll tell you what," he said. "Tomorrow is meant to be a nice day. I'm at work but why don't you and Mum try a ride together?"

"Err...'cos of my a..." Amber began in a rather bemused tone.

"Yes, I know, but it's almost healed now. If Mum has you on a lead-rein and you just go for a little walk, I'm sure it'll be fine. Pearlipops will look after you, won't she?"

And so the next day, which was cold but sunny as predicted, Mrs Anderson helped Amber to mount Pearl gingerly from the mounting block in the yard. She adjusted the stirrups, handed Amber the reins, plus an additional lead-rope she'd clipped to Pearl's bit, and made sure Amber was as comfortable as possible before bringing Molly out and mounting herself. Then she took hold of Pearl's leading rein and they walked side by side out of the yard.

Pearl struggled to walk alongside Molly, with her much longer stride, so the leading rein was lengthened to allow Pearl to go at her own pace. There was no wind but the raw air nibbled Amber's cheeks and ears and burrowed under her gloves to stiffen her fingers. It was a joy to be back out riding again and normally she didn't mind the cold too much as a good brisk trot was usually enough to keep warm, but with Amber's arm still in its sling, they had to remain in walk.

"My toes are turning a bit numb, how about you?" her mum shouted over her shoulder as they approached the forestry gate.

"Yeah, me too."

"Shall we turn around here then and go back?"

"Okay."

Molly seemed delighted that her ride had been cut short so early and appeared to remember her recent gallop all the way home from the gate when she left Amber on the ground. She started to jog and snatch the reins from Mrs Anderson's frozen fingers. As she jigged sideways and continued to pull the reins in her attempt to break from walk, Molly managed to cause Mrs Anderson to drop Pearl's lead-rope.

"Oh, damn it! Walk you blasted thing!" Mrs Anderson sat deep in the saddle and hunched her shoulders, doing her 'sack of taties' impression that she knew was often the best way to calm a tense pony down. "I'm sorry Amber, I daren't let go of her to get hold of your lead-rope. Are you okay?"

"I'm fine," Amber assured her. Pearl, as ever, was paying no attention whatsoever to the fine display of impromptu dressage movements being performed in front of her, and continued to amble along peacefully. Amber had managed to pull the lead-rope up so it wasn't dangling down and getting dragged along the ground and had it draped over Pearl's neck. She only had one hand to steer with, but Pearl knew her way home.

As they turned back on to the farm track, Molly seemed to lose interest in all the prancing and piaffe she was performing and went back to a walk. Relieved, Mrs Anderson relaxed and turned around to check on Amber, who at that moment was day-dreaming about being like Jo – having the ability to do tumble turns and beautiful no-bump French plaits. It was also at this moment that

Pearl decided she had an itch on the right side of her face. Normally, she'd just fling out a foreleg, come to an abrupt halt, and rub her face on her leg to get rid of the itch, but today, Molly's bottom was conveniently placed just in front of her. Pearl shoved her head against Molly's left hip and rubbed vigorously.

The next moments seemed to happen in slow motion. Molly pinned her ears back in annoyance, Amber tried to pull Pearl away with her left hand and her mother rose higher in the air as Molly's left hind leg shot out like a piston to remove the sudden irritation that had startled her. Her steel-shod shoe missed Pearl and landed squarely against Amber's right knee.

"AAARRRGGHHHH!" she screamed in agony.

"Oh! Oh, are you alright?" Her mother's colourless face now had nothing to do with the cold.

Amber couldn't answer. Her brain throbbed in time with her knee as pain shot through her like a rollercoaster. She squeezed her eyes closed tightly and moaned, trying not to let another scream escape her. When she opened them again and looked at her right knee, she could see it had already begun to swell.

By the time they reached the farmyard, all discomfort from numb fingers and toes had been forgotten and the tears had broken through. Amber's knee was so swollen she couldn't bend her leg, and between that and her arm, it had been almost impossible to get her off Pearl.

Caroline Blakely had been summoned from the farmhouse once more to attend to Molly while Mrs Anderson hurriedly threw Pearl back into the field with Honey and rushed Amber to the hospital.

Again.

- Nine -

New Year's Resolution

The New Year began dismally with rain fattened, bruised clouds glowering in the sky each day. Occasionally, their hostility was softened by a trimming of gold as the sun tried to sneak around their plump outlines, but it was always pushed back and never allowed to break through the oppressive ranks of grey.

There was never anything good about January. Christmas festivities were over, school was beginning again and the days were short and dull, punctuated with regular downpours of rain, hail or sleet. There was Amber's thirteenth birthday on the eighth, which she'd been shocked to discover she shared with Jo, but even this was spoiled by the fact that it fell on a Tuesday that year, meaning she'd spend most of it at school fighting with physics, food tech, history, IT and German.

Amber's hopes for the new year were modest: no more pony disappointments or disasters, and no more injuries. She knew she needed to start riding Molly again to see if the pony had benefited from her six month 'no jumping' period, but the thought filled her with dread. When she'd won a show jumping class with Molly last year, she'd been so full of hope for the fun and success they were going to have. She'd imagined other riders pointing them out and saying, "Oh no, Amber and Molly are in this class. They're the ones to beat."

But then Molly had stopped jumping and the 'back man' and vet hadn't been able to find anything physically wrong with her that could be affecting her performance. The Andersons had been advised to give her a period of rest and relaxation to see if that would help but Amber had an uncomfortable feeling that it could be her own poor riding that had caused Molly's sudden reluctance as she'd been used to a confident, experienced rider before she became Amber's. Added to that was the fact that Molly had also bolted with her, thrown her and broken her collarbone, and kicked her in the knee which had resulted in the most painful procedure of Amber's life involving a huge needle to drain the fluid that enlarged her knee to the size of a football.

With Natalie out show jumping successfully on a pony Amber never thought she'd be able to manage, Amber felt even more pressure to get going with her own *proven show jumper*, knowing that people would be wondering what had happened to the wonderful Just Molly since she'd left the Drake family. But how was she supposed to get over her mistrust of Molly? If just the thought of her made Amber's insides shiver, how was she supposed to get back in the saddle? Molly would feel her fear and that would make both of them nervous and unhappy.

At least there was the tetrathlon to focus on, with the Brantfort branch competition taking place in May.

The postal shoot was nearly over and Amber had ended up shooting all of her targets left-handed after all. She'd waited to get her sling off so she could use her right hand, but her arm felt so weak, she could barely lift it. In contrast, her left side had become much stronger as she'd been forced to do everything with it, and her grip was now fiercely firm from all the frustrated squeezing of the blue stress ball.

When she'd gone for her first competitive round of targets, she'd tried lifting the gun shakily with her right arm and Mr Jones had noticed she was closing her right eye.

"You need to close your left eye and use your right when you're shooting right-handed," he'd instructed her, thinking she'd just got used to looking through the sights with her left eye during her left-handed practice.

"I can't close my left eye."

"What do you mean, you can't close your left eye? Everyone can close both their eyes!" He closed his eyes one by one to demonstrate.

"No," she said, willing her left eye to close but getting no response. "I just can't!"

"Oh. Well…in that case…you'll either have to wear a patch over your left eye or…shoot left-handed."

And so, armed with a new pair of glasses so she could actually see what she was aiming at, she'd shot, left-handed, nine targets out of the twelve required, and was getting better all the time. Her last three had even contained several shots in the bullseye.

Now that Christmas was over, she was due to start training for the running and swimming phases of the tetrathlon with everyone else who had put their names forward to be on a team, in either the minimus, junior or senior age groups. Emily had sensed Amber's reluctance to attend the training after she'd expressed an interest in running the forestry tracks with Jo instead. Her own dad was pretty sporty, playing competitive badminton and having run some half marathons in the past. She was sure he'd be able to help them if needed, but how hard could it be? It was only running after all. There was no skill involved, she just needed to be fitter to cope with the distance. But Emily had pleaded with Amber to come with her for moral support. She seemed pretty convinced she was going to get a hard time from her dad.

The running couldn't start yet as it was still too dark after school and everyone was busy with their ponies at weekends, but the swimming was due to start that month on Friday evenings at the local pool, whenever there wasn't a stable management rally. Amber was determined to try her hardest to match the performance of the other team members; she didn't want to be the weakest link whose score ended up being discounted. *This isn't just a riding competition, she thought to herself, this is so much more. I've got a real chance to be as good as everyone else in the other three phases if I work hard enough.*

Amber looked forward to beginning the training, hoping this might be her chance to shine.

- Jen -

Pride

When Amber entered the changing room, she found Emily and Chelsea already in their swimming costumes waiting for her. *So Chelsea is the fourth member* she thought. *Jo will be pleased.*

The minimus swimmers were about to finish, with the juniors and seniors going next. Amber already had her costume on so she hurriedly peeled off her clothes and rammed them into a locker while sneaking a look at her teammates.

Emily was, as she herself admitted, unusually proportioned with her long back and short, stumpy legs. *But*, thought Amber, *although this might be a disadvantage in the running, it was unlikely to affect her in the swimming.* Chelsea, on the other hand, was built like an athlete. Although she wasn't tall, she was perfectly compact. Her arms and legs were well muscled, giving her a powerful appearance. When Amber compared her own skinny arms and legs to Chelsea's, she doubted she'd match her for athletic ability. Jo had already reported on her own super swimming skills, complete with tumble turns, so Amber's hope that this could be her phase dimmed. It was likely to be between her and Emily as to who was the weakest. She shook her head, seeking to dislodge the thought before it took root. She'd learned her lesson about being jealous of friends some time ago. It was no good and she didn't want to go there again. They were teammates after all. Although they'd be competing against each other for individual placings, they were also working together for the team section of the competition. She had to learn to see their strengths as hers. But there was always that little voice in her head muttering about letting everyone down that nagged at her insistently and made her doubt herself.

The three girls, along with some older members who were in the senior group, made their way to the pool and began warming up. Everyone else stuck to breaststroke but Amber found front crawl easier so pulled her goggles on and did a few leisurely lengths before she had to stop to get her breath back. Just as she was resting in the shallow end, the strident blare of a whistle echoed in her water-filled ears.

"Swimmers, to me!"

Turning around, she saw that Emily's dad was standing behind her. He wore flip-flops, shorts and a vest, which showed off his unusually tanned muscles, considering it was January and everyone else resembled milk bottles. A whistle and stopwatch hung around his bulging neck.

Once all the swimmers had congregated, he addressed them, looking down at their heads bobbing in the water.

"So, both juniors and seniors – you have to swim for three minutes with the distance you cover in that time being measured. You'll score points according to how far you've swum. We're going to cover a range of techniques to build your stamina and increase your speed. To begin with, I want to assess where you are now as a starting point, so…everyone out!"

The girls looked at each other uncertainly. Emily rolled her eyes at Amber.

"Come on! Out you get." He bent down and clapped his hands at them. "I want you to walk up to the deep end and line up. We're going to have a race."

There was a quiet groan as the girls either slithered out of the shallow end on their tummies or swam to the steps and climbed out. They traipsed to the deep end and lined up as instructed, dripping as they curled their toes around the edge of the pool.

"Right ladies. When you hear the whistle, I want you to dive in and swim two lengths as fast as you can. The first to get back here is the winner!" His eyes flashed as he brought the whistle to his lips. The girls pulled their goggles over their eyes and moved into position, ready to dive.

Amber was the last girl to enter the water but she kicked hard and swam as fast as she could, only noticing the other swimmers as she turned her head to breathe. She reached the shallow end and turned, pushing off the wall with force, propelling herself back up her lane. *I'm not last!* She could see she had overtaken some of the other girls. Soon her outstretched hand touched the wall of the deep end, signalling the end of her race. Her heart felt like it was going to jump out of her mouth and her breath exploded from her in a mighty roar; for the last few metres she'd held her breath as she powered towards the finish.

She lifted her left arm and rested her elbow on the edge of the pool, pushing her goggles onto her forehead, just as the last of the girls were finishing.

"Seniors: first – Elise, second – Maia, third – Katie, fourth – Isobel. Juniors: first – Chelsea, second – Amber, third – Emily."

Emily was holding onto the wall, pointedly not looking at her father.

"That was a great swim from Chelsea, who was the overall winner, and Elise, and good competitive spirit was shown by Amber, who, after a bad start, caught up and finished very strongly." Amber was incredulous to receive a compliment and felt a flash of pride crackle through her like electricity. Her eyes flicked to where her dad was sitting in the nearby viewing gallery wondering if he could hear her being praised. "I'll let you get your breaths back and swim some lengths at your own pace, then we'll repeat it at the end."

The hour passed quite quickly, with each girl swimming individually while Mr Pryde shouted encouraging or instructive comments at them like, "nice smooth strokes Katie", "turn your head as your arm is passing under the water Isobel" and "kick faster Emily. Use those legs more!"

At one point, Emily had tried to have a chat with Amber as they both took a rest in the shallow end, but Mr Pryde was soon there clapping at them and harassing them into getting moving again.

In the second race, Amber was determined not to be left behind at the start. It felt good to have her efforts recognised in the first race and she was keen to give an even better performance. The whistle gave the signal to go and Amber reacted, but somehow, she was still the last one to launch herself into the pool. Again, she fought against the water, pulling herself gracefully along as if her life depended on it. She still didn't beat Chelsea but she came fourth overall, beating two of the senior girls. The praise she'd received seemed to have given her extra power. Poor Emily finished last again.

"That's it, girls. That's the end," Mr Pryde informed them after he'd imparted the results of the race. "See you all next week. Next time you'll be swimming for three minutes to test your stamina. That's what you need – speed and stamina if you're going to be winners!"

Back in the changing room, Amber shyly congratulated Chelsea for winning both of the races.

"Thanks. You seemed to do quite well yourself," she replied, squeezing water out of her stumpy brown ponytail.

"Yeah, when it's only two lengths. The test will be next week when we have to do three minutes."

"I know. It doesn't sound like very long, but I bet it feels like forever when you're doing it."

"Yeah, I bet!"

Amber was about to say more to Chelsea, to try and get to know their final team member better, but Emily had dressed quickly and looked like she was going to leave. Amber turned her attention away from Chelsea and called after her.

"Em, wait! Give me a minute and I'll walk out with you." Amber was struggling with her socks as her feet were still damp. Emily slouched against the lockers as Chelsea gave a cheery, "Bye, see you next week" and left, the door banging loudly as she swung it with more force than was necessary. "Oops," she laughed as the door whacked against the wall.

Reading Emily's slumped shoulders and unsmiling face, Amber knew she was upset about finishing last in both the races. It could be that speed wasn't her friend's forte, but maybe she'd do better with distance. Amber considered saying this in the hope it might cheer her up, but decided to change the subject instead.

"How's Pink?"

It was the right choice. Emily's face lit up. "Oh, she's funny. Some days she seems really pleased to see me, but other days it's all ears back and grumpy faces. Poor Fudgey is terrified of her. She's definitely the boss. I think she's bored and wants to get out of the stable more, but our little field is just a mud bath at the moment so they can't go out. She's bonkers at the weekend when I ride her. I'm supposed to be looking after Harry but he's having to fend for himself. It's okay though 'cos Fudge never puts a foot wrong."

With Emily restored to her usual ebullient self, the girls chatted about their ponies as they walked to the reception area where their dads stood waiting for them, deep in conversation.

"They're probably discussing marathons," Amber joked.

"Wait…is your dad into all that too?" Emily grabbed Amber's arm, making her stop in her tracks.

"Well…sort of. He's quite sporty and he's done marathons in the past."

"Oh! You're in the same boat as me then." Emily chuckled, seeming pleased. "We can weather the storm together."

As Emily bounced merrily towards the two men, Amber followed uneasily. If Emily thought that her dad was going to join in with training or would start getting her up at 5.30am for pre-school runs, she was mistaken. She'd never thought about it before, but her dad was a competitive person, yet he didn't force that part of his personality onto her. She had never been pushed into trying to win anything in her life. She thought about school sports days where some parents had their children in tears because they hadn't done well in their races. Amber herself had always been terrible in any race she was entered for in sports day, but her parents had never failed to congratulate her for her efforts.

Emily seemed to have a premonition that her father was going to be disappointed in her and would push her to be the least disappointing she could be. As Amber got into the car beside her own father, it occurred to her for the first time that maybe *he* was disappointed in *her*…but just didn't show it. She took after her mother and shared many of the same strengths and weaknesses as her, but all the things her dad was good at, like sport, maths and science, she had no affinity with at all.

She looked at him as he was watching for cars at the pool's exit junction and wondered…*what does he really think of me?*

And in that moment, Amber determined, she was going to do everything she could to make him proud of her…in case he wasn't already.

- Eleven -

The Molly Mission

Spring arrived quietly. There was no fanfare or spotlight moment. The sun just gently, gradually nudged the obese clouds aside until there was room for it to stretch and reach out with warm, nurturing fingers to coax buds into flowers and turn the brown fields green again.

The warmer, longer days meant that riding was no longer confined just to weekends. Having spent the winter months watching all of Natalie's posts about her and Elisha's success on the winter show jumping circuit, Amber was determined to conquer her fear of Molly.

She'd started by going out with her parents. The forestry gate had been fitted with a spring-loaded closing mechanism, which meant it was now impossible to negotiate without dismounting and remounting. There was no way she could trust Molly with that yet, so she always had company.

Once she'd built her confidence riding with her parents, she started to venture out with Jo and Matthew. Jo had no problems mounting Merry, who stood like a rock for her rider to climb aboard. Sometimes she and Matthew were asked to trot away so that Merry would follow them, allowing Jo to practise vaulting on. Although Jo had only recently turned twelve, she'd grown again and could vault on the 14.2hh pony easily.

At first, they'd just walked and trotted, with Amber gripping the reins tightly, expecting Molly to launch herself into a flat-out gallop at any moment. But their early rides passed without incident and Amber's iron fists started to soften.

Next, they introduced some canters up the forestry hill. Jo and Matthew stayed well back so that Molly didn't think it was a race, and the incline of the hill was used to tire her out. Once it became apparent that Molly was under control, Amber was able to thrill at the power of her long stride and the ease with which she flew up the hill without breaking a sweat or getting out of breath.

Gradually, canters in other places were introduced. Molly was always allowed to set off first, just in case, but although she clearly enjoyed stretching her legs, she remained calm and showed no signs of bolting. Amber's confidence began to blossom like a trembling flower unfurling its petals and she was able to once again marvel at the gleaming golden neck and long, pricked ears in front of her. As the fragile trust between them began to strengthen, Amber became more daring.

One day, as they prepared for their canter up the hill, an exciting idea crept into Amber's mind and sent a shiver of anticipation coursing through her.

"Jo… can we try something?" she called over her shoulder to her friend who was in her usual position behind Molly.

"Yeah, what?"

"Once we set off, can you let Merry catch up instead of keeping her behind?"

A broad grin lit up Jo's face. "You want to let them gallop?"

"Yeah." Amber couldn't believe she was even suggesting it, never mind looking forward to it.

"Awesome!" Jo clearly approved of the plan.

Molly seemed to understand Amber's words and began to jog on the spot, waiting to be released. The pony's energy infected Amber and she couldn't wait to begin. As she leaned forward and let the reins slip fractionally through her fingers, Molly flowed forward immediately like water bursting from a dam. A thrill of fear electrified Amber, but this time it was good fear, like how it felt to ride cross-country, tackling the imposing, solid fences.

Molly flew like an arrow released from a bow, but Merry's head soon appeared alongside Amber's leg. Jo was crouched over the palomino like a jockey, not letting the pony pick her own pace, but urging her on. *She's trying to race us*, Amber thought. Her brain flicked through images of the last pony race that Jo had been involved in. It had ended in hospitalisation for Jo and horrendous injuries to her pony, Flash, when the race went wrong. Amber instinctively drew back on her reins. Perhaps she was worried for herself, or maybe it was out of concern for Jo, but Molly tugged back, not wanting to be stopped. Amber looked over at Jo, still racing beside her, and a competitive streak suddenly flared within her. At the end of Pony Club camp last summer, she had declared to Emily that winning didn't matter to her so long as she felt she'd done her best, but in that moment, the need to win was fierce. Although Jo had looked after her during their rides, never been impatient, or criticised her lack of confidence, she was always a competitor…and she liked to win. Amber accepted the challenge.

"Go on girl!" she yelled into the wind. If she thought Molly had been going fast before, that was nothing compared to what happened next. Molly shot forward as if she'd been fired out of a catapult, leaving Amber breathless. She saw Jo riding hard to keep up but Molly was not going to be caught. By the time Amber pulled her mount up at the top of the hill, they were well clear of their rivals, and for the first time, Molly's sides were heaving with exertion. Amber patted her ecstatically. After all the times trailing behind Jo on the Fell ponies, she felt so proud of Molly. It was funny; this was no competition really, but Amber felt as if she'd won a gold medal.

"That was amazing!" Jo's face was flushed and her blue eyes seemed electrified as she drew level with Amber. They both brought their ponies to a halt to wait for Matthew to catch up on Sam and let the ponies recover.

"I know! I can't believe we did that."

"You can't? I couldn't believe that you suggested it. We'll be able to have great fun now with these two."

Matthew had appeared on Sam, who was dripping with sweat. He was scowling, no doubt unimpressed with being left so far behind by the bigger ponies. Amber gave him a sympathetic smile – she knew exactly how he felt – but he didn't smile back. They waited a few moments longer for Sam to get his breath back, then they set off for home. Sam trudged along at the back but Molly and Merry appeared to be continuing their race in walk as they matched each other stride for stride back along the lane.

"I'm sorry I beat you," Amber said. She wasn't sorry at all, but it seemed like the best thing to say in case Jo went into a sulk about it. But to Amber's surprise, I-like-to-win-Jo wasn't dismayed.

"Ahh, you won today but there'll be other days and other races. I'm just really pleased that you two are getting on again and you can start to enjoy her now. I don't know if she's done much, or any, cross-country jumping before. The Drake's only did show jumping and gymkhanas as

94

far as I know, but with that speed, she'll be brilliant. When are you going to start jumping her again?"

Amber's joy dampened at the mention of jumping. It was one thing to sit on a pony's back and let it run fast, but jumping required skilled and confident riding. She was still sure, since there seemed to be nothing wrong with Molly physically, that her bad riding must have been the cause of Molly's poor performance last year. She dreaded trying again in case the same thing happened and confirmed that she was a terrible rider who couldn't handle a good pony. *But don't forget*, the voice in her head reminded her, *you've done so well with Honey. You can't be that bad a rider to have achieved what you have on a pony like her*. But Amber didn't listen. She was so used to the voice in her head telling her things she didn't want to hear; she didn't notice when it was telling her something good for once.

"Erm, I don't know. Soon," she replied, bluntly.

- Twelve -

Candle in the Wind

With two months left until the tetrathlon, it was time for running training to begin. And for pony training.

Although there was no doubt in Amber's mind that she would be riding Honey in the tetrathlon, she knew that she couldn't keep putting off trying to jump with Molly again. All her friends had their own competition ponies, and she needed to get to grips with hers to avoid getting left behind...and to make her parents' investment in her and Molly worth it. Honey was great, but she'd been so good, out of nowhere and with no training, Amber knew that it had nothing to do with her. Honey would be good with anyone...but she was just good. She had limits that Molly didn't have. But Molly was used to skilled riding whereas Honey had had a lifetime of novice riders, so, to her, Amber probably seemed like a blessing.

The Pony Club had shown her that there was far more to riding effectively than she had ever thought possible. In order for a pony to perform well, it needed a driver, not a passenger. Amber had to swallow her pride and accept that she still had a lot to learn if she wanted to develop a partnership with Molly.

Pony Club rallies were great for building trust, but they were not frequent enough. Claire was asked about resuming lessons again, but she was far too busy with her own ponies and the riding school to fit Amber in. Her parents considered asking Rachel Best, their Pony Club DC's daughter if she could offer some private tuition, until Mr Anderson had the brainwave of asking Caroline.

Despite Oriel's lumpy knees and disfigured face, she looked a picture of health. Her muscles were hard and laced with a network of veins, her coat was lustrous and the horse seemed to be bursting with energy. Yet, when Caroline rode her, she was always beautifully well-mannered and appeared to obey every invisible command through telepathy as Caroline's riding was so quiet, her aids were imperceptible. Watching her schooling the big, powerful horse in the paddock one day, while Amber and her mother were out riding, Mr Anderson had a great idea.

As Caroline dismounted and led Oriel towards the paddock gate, Mr Anderson congratulated her on the session. Caroline looked up and blushed, startled by his voice. She hadn't known she was being watched.

"She's going great. It's amazing that such a big horse can move so lightly," he complimented her, pulling the gate open. Caroline looked down, mumbling something that he couldn't make out. "Would you...we're looking for someone to help Amber with Molly," he began. "Her mother and I are fine with the hacking but we've never done any schooling or jumping so we can't be any use with that. Would you be interested in giving her some lessons?"

Caroline looked aghast at the suggestion; her face resembled a mottled plum. "Oh no, I couldn't. I'm not a qualified instructor."

"Pah!" Mr Anderson snorted. "That doesn't matter. You're a brilliant rider. And you do it so quietly, so gently too. You and Oriel work together, you're a team – there's no fighting or force – and that's the way Amber wants to ride."

Caroline looked as if she might cry. "I...I...don't know." Her voice was barely a whisper. "I don't know if I could."

"No pressure. Just think about it. Maybe try one and see how it goes. We could go from there."

The next evening after school, Amber rode Molly into the paddock for her first lesson with Caroline. Her mum had brought her through but tactfully stayed away, knowing that neither Caroline nor Amber would appreciate an audience.

It began with Caroline giving some tentative instructions that Amber could barely hear but she did what she thought she was being asked. Seeing Amber respond to her suggestions, the young woman gradually grew in confidence, and her commands became more audible. After a while, Caroline, watching Molly's movement shrewdly, asked Amber to stop. She walked towards her and reached up to the saddle, feeling around it, sliding her fingers under the seat and the pommel.

"This saddle is feeling a bit tight," she said, so quietly, Amber had to lean forward to hear her. "I think she's put on some weight since you got her, and this could be pinching her. She doesn't look comfortable to me. I'd say this could do with being checked by a saddler before you start doing much more with her. We'll stop there for today."

"Okay, I'll tell Mum and Dad. Thanks for the lesson."

Caroline's gaze slipped away over Molly's shoulder and she smiled.

***

"A saddler now?" her mother exclaimed. "She's had a vet and an osteopath and now she needs a saddler! What next? A dentist? A hairdresser? A therapist? Caroline said that saddle fit her – that's why we bought it."

"She said it fit her a year ago. Molly's put on weight, so it needs checked to see if it still fits. And yes, horses do need dentists too." Amber replied, delivering the news when her mother enquired about the lesson on the drive home.

"Hmph! And where do we find a saddler? Did Caroline tell you that?"

"No." Amber almost wished she hadn't passed Caroline's advice on. Her mother didn't seem pleased, probably because it would be another possibly fruitless expense since the vet and osteopath visits hadn't found anything to explain Molly's behaviour. "I'm sure we could ask around and find out. Maybe her saddle isn't comfortable for her and that's why she's been behaving as she has. It's worth getting it checked out?"

A spark of hope flickered deep within Amber. The saddle could be the true root of the problems which might mean it wasn't *her* the pony objected to, but the discomfort she felt while being ridden. It was like a candle flame at the end of a long, dark tunnel, shivering in a cold wind.

"Yes, well, I suppose we'd better get it checked out and get a dentist out too while we're at it, but don't get your hopes up. It might not be the answer you're hoping for." Her mother seemed to read her mind. Amber didn't reply. The candle flame wavered hesitantly, but it didn't go out.

– Thirteen –

Marlyn

A saddler was soon found through recommendations from Mrs Best, and as she was visiting the area for some other appointments, they didn't have to wait long. She was able to fit them in at 2pm on a Monday, if they could bring Molly to a livery yard near Cockermouth to be seen after the other horses on the yard.

Both of Amber's parents happened to be off work on that day, so they could take her, but Amber wasn't happy that the appointment would take place while she was at school.

"I've only got P.E and chemistry period 4 and 5 on Monday. Couldn't you make up a dentist appointment or something for me so I can be there?" she pleaded.

She could tell her mother wanted to say no, but if she did, how would Amber get home from school? There would be no-one to pick her up if they were both dealing with Molly and who knew where they'd be at 3.15pm?

"I don't think it's a good idea for you to miss chemistry, love. Mr Tippet said at parents evening that you find it quite difficult and…"

"Urgh. God, Mum, I'm only in Year Eight," Amber interrupted. "It's not like I've got my GCSE's this year – they're *three years* away. I can copy Sarah's notes and see if there's any homework in chemistry?" She lightened her voice and put her hands together in prayer, looking at her mother with the same expression Kasper, their cocker spaniel, used for begging.

"Oh, well, alright then!"

And so, at 1.30 pm on Monday, Amber was collected from school for her 'dentist' appointment in the family estate car with a trailer attached, and her pony in tow. If any teachers had witnessed it, they would certainly have been puzzled.

Marlyn, the saddler was a tall wiry woman with a shock of Albert Einstein-esque white hair which framed her smooth, serene face like a dandelion clock. She worked briskly but not unkindly, taking templates of Molly's withers and inspecting her current saddle. She quickly declared it unsuitable for Molly's shape.

"She's a slim pony with a high wither, but she has quite a broad spine and a big shoulder. This saddle doesn't accommodate them," she stated, matter-of-factly, whisking the saddle from Molly's back like it was an irritating fly.

Amber's face was a contradiction of emotions. Her eyes gleamed with the hope that the saddle, not her, could have been the cause of their problems, but her teeth clenched and her jaw hardened at the thought that poor Molly had been suffering for all this time with a pain she couldn't tell them about in any other way than through her behaviour. If only they'd thought to get the saddle checked sooner.

"That's not good news," Mr Anderson said from where he stood in the barn doorway. It was a drizzly day so Molly had been brought inside the large barn for her fitting. Horses and ponies of all sizes and colours reached out over their internal stable doors to inspect the newcomer. Molly's ears flicked and her nostrils quivered in the new surroundings, but she stood very still as Amber held her, out of reach of inquisitive noses. "What does that mean? A new one?"

Amber knew that her father would be worried about the cost. She'd seen some saddles advertised in that month's PONY magazine and noted that they cost thousands of pounds brand new.

"Well, she can't keep wearing the one she's got..." Marlyn replied. "I've got lots of saddles in the van. We can try a few and see what fits, then you can decide what you want to do."

With brisk efficiency, a range of saddles were brought out and tried. Some were immediately discarded; some took a few minutes of examination before also being dismissed until there were just two that were deemed suitable.

"I need to have a rider on board now to check the fit again and see how Molly moves in them. And," she added, "it's important that the rider also feels comfortable."

Amber had already changed out of her school uniform into her riding clothes, so she put on her hat and bridled Molly before mounting her to try the first selected saddle. Once Marlyn had approved the fit with a rider on board, Amber was asked to ride Molly around in the yard's outdoor arena.

She could feel the difference immediately. Molly moved forward much more freely and Amber had to check her pace with several half halts to slow her down. She felt so much more secure. This saddle had a smaller, deeper seat with a higher cantle than on the one she had. It held her in place so snugly, she realised how much she'd been slipping around in the old one – an image of a garden pea rolling around in a teaspoon came to mind.

She was grinning when she dismounted to swap the saddles to try Marlyn's second selection. Molly still went well in the second saddle but Amber didn't like it half as much. It didn't give her the feeling of security she'd got from the first one. When asked for her appraisal of the saddles, she chose the first one without hesitation, even though it was black and didn't look as good on Molly as the second one, which was a gleaming conker colour and matched Molly's chestnut coat perfectly.

Marlyn agreed that it was the best choice for both of them and Amber's heart leapt…until Marlyn revealed its price. Two thousand pounds. Mr and Mrs Anderson looked at each other without speaking. Amber knew they were wondering how to tell Marlyn, and her, that it was more than they could afford.

Interpreting the silence, Marlyn said, while putting the cover back on the second saddle, "I know it's a lot of money, but a pony can't do its work in a saddle that doesn't fit."

"Yes, I know, but..." Mrs Anderson started.

"She'll have to make do with something cheaper," Amber blurted out. The disappointment of seeing all her hopes being taken away pulled the trigger and fired the words unchecked.

"Amber!"

The shock in her father's voice made Amber lower her head.

"Sorry," she muttered, embarrassed by her outburst.

"But," Marlyn cut in, "you don't have to have a new one. I've got one just like the one Amber preferred coming in next week in a part exchange. It's brown and a few years old, so it'll be almost half the price of the new one." She slammed the back doors of the van closed and shook the Andersons' hands. "Have a think about it and let me know."

Amber's mother nodded at her father silently and replied with, "No, it's okay. Even we could see the difference in both of them with that saddle, so we'll take it… the second hand one."

A deposit was paid to reserve the saddle and Marlyn even took Molly's current saddle in part exchange there and then, since she advised them not to use it again. Amber was elated and looked forward to a fresh start with Molly. This saddle could be the key to the brilliant future she'd imagined when Molly became hers.

– Fourteen –

Run

Back at the farm, Amber thanked Caroline for her advice and enthusiastically told her all about the 'new' saddle she would be getting next week.

"I can't ride her until the saddle comes but it would be great if you could give me some more lessons when it does." Amber didn't usually like to ask for anything but she admired Caroline's riding and liked her quiet manner. Instructors often had a tendency to roar at riders if they didn't do what they said immediately, but Caroline was patient and didn't have a shout in her. Amber was happy to ask Caroline to explain or repeat her instructions without feeling intimidated.

Not meeting Amber's eyes, Caroline replied, "There are some activities you could do with her from the ground. I could show you if you like? They're good for building your relationship and would give you something to do with her while you can't ride."

Amber was keen to take up Caroline's offer, so on Thursday after school, she chased her parents off on a ride on the Fell ponies while she went to work with Molly in the paddock with Caroline. She felt better with no-one watching.

Caroline explained how to use slight body language signals to get Molly to walk beside her when she asked, stop when Amber stopped, back up and turn. Molly, however, seemed to ignore Amber's signals, leaving her disheartened. Molly clearly didn't understand this silent language that Caroline was talking about.

"She can't do it!" Amber huffed, throwing her whip into the grass at her feet. She'd stepped towards Molly with a whip held out horizontally in front of her. According to Caroline, this was meant to make the pony move away from her, but Molly just looked bored and didn't budge.

Without speaking, Caroline stepped into Amber's place, quietly took the lead-rope and picked the whip up. Standing tall, she locked eyes on Molly and stepped towards her confidently, whip held out in front of her, parallel to the ground. Molly immediately took a calm, unhurried step away. Caroline paused, lowered her eyes, then began again. She and the pony were soon involved in a silent dance that moved forward, back and sideways without a single word uttered. Amber was spellbound. It wasn't Molly who couldn't understand this language – clearly, it was she who couldn't speak it. Unlike Caroline, who was fluent. Amber guessed that Caroline was much happier communicating with horses in their silent language than she was with interacting with people.

Watching Caroline with her pony made her determined to master this secret language, so, instead of sulking, she listened attentively and tried hard to copy what Caroline showed her. Molly didn't react to her as well as she had to Caroline but the young woman assured Amber that progress could be made if she practised, was patient, and kept her signals clear and consistent.

"You could try making an L shape with poles on the ground and get her to go forwards and backwards through it – it's harder than it sounds," Caroline suggested. "Or make a washing line between those two trees, hang some towels or rugs from it and get her to follow you under them. It's good for building her trust in you."

Desperate to impress Caroline, who was becoming her idol, Amber practised some more with Molly back in the stable while she waited to hear the sound of hooves in the yard that signalled her parents' return. She gave Molly her feed, laughing at the way the pony always ate her feed standing on three legs. For some reason, she always bent her left foreleg at the knee and ate the entire contents of her bucket with her left hoof in her armpit. Still chuckling at this odd foible, Amber left Molly's stable and went to help untack and brush the Fell ponies before giving them a hug and kiss on the nose and turning them back out into their field.

Over the weekend, Amber was kept busy. As well as riding Honey and Pearl and doing Molly's in-hand groundwork activities, there was also Saturday morning running to do.

Now that days were getting longer, giving everyone more time to fit their busy lives in before darkness fell, Mr Pryde had introduced running training every Saturday. It went straight from Emily's house as a cycle path passed behind their field and could be accessed by hopping over their field fence – after waiting for the electric current to be turned off first so that a nasty shock wasn't received.

The littlies went first – AKA the minimus group – who had to run 1,000 metres. Then the junior and senior groups were together as with swimming, because both age groups had 1,500 metres to run.

At school, Amber was a decent runner at 400 and 800 metres. She wasn't a good sprinter as she wasn't fast enough off the mark, and she wasn't good at distances. Like Honey, she lacked the stamina. But at 400 and 800 metres, Amber could build her speed gradually and hold on at the end where lots of the shorter distance specialists tired and faded away. 1,500 metres was further than she was comfortable with but at least the cycle path was a smooth and mainly flat surface.

Emily was stony-faced as they climbed tentatively over her field fence and did some stretches while they waited for Mr Pryde to appear. There was no Chelsea or Jo but Elise, Maia and Isobel – three of the four senior girls – were all warming up too.

Just as Amber was about to start filling Emily in on her Molly news, Mr Pryde leapt over the fence like a hurdler, wearing a pair of tiny white shorts that did little to cover his bulging thighs, and a loose black t-shirt.

"Right girls!" He hopped on the spot, waggling his arms by his sides, "I've measured out to a point 1,600 metres down the track and marked it with some baling twine tied to a tree on either side so you'll see the end."

"But…we only have to run 1,500 metres, don't we?" asked Maia, looking stricken.

"You do, but you should always train at a level higher than required in competition. If you train over a mile, 1,500 metres on the day will seem easier. Okay then. When I say go, I want you all to set off as fast as you can and sprint for as long as you can. I know you won't be able to keep that pace up 'til the end, but even if you slow down, you'll still be going faster than if you start slow and try to build up as you go."

Amber looked at Emily and pursed her lips. That wasn't how she ran. She was never fast off the mark – her strength was in building up and finishing strongly. She couldn't see this method working for her, but she didn't dare tell Mr Pryde.

And so, the girls formed two starting lines: the three senior girls followed by Amber and Emily.

"On your marks," Mr Pryde called, "get set…go!"

The girls moved off as instructed – fast. Amber struggled immediately as her ankles felt like they'd locked, causing her to hop a few steps to get them working again.

"Come on Amber! Faster," Mr Pryde yelled at her as the others pulled away and left her behind. Afraid to refuse, Amber surged forward and soon caught up with Emily, then Maia, but Elise and Isobel were still well ahead. Elise and Isobel managed to keep going until they collapsed at the marked ending, but the other girls – Amber included – were barely jogging by the time they reached the finishing point.

She folded over like a sapling in a storm, her chest heaving as she clutched her knees and waited for her breathing to return to a steady pace. Beside her, Emily was doing the same, but with one hand pressed against her stomach, fighting the urge to puke.

"Are…you…okay?" Amber panted. Emily didn't acknowledge her, but continued holding her stomach while her breath rasped in and out.

Mr Pryde wasn't remotely out of breath and continued jogging on the spot while he waited for the girls to recover.

"I think we need to work on fitness," he said, stating the obvious. "We'll do some interval training on the way back. Walk 100 metres, jog 100 metres, sprint 100 metres, then repeat. Okay. Come on, let's start walking back."

"How did that go?" Mrs Anderson asked when Amber returned to the house where her mother had been having a coffee with Mrs Pryde.

"Horrendous. Oh sorry!" Amber hadn't noticed Emily's mum in the utility room.

"Don't mind me, love, I know what he's like. He'll train you like Olympians!"

"Let's hope you win the gold then," Mrs Anderson replied, rescuing Amber.

- Fifteen -

A Difficult Choice

Easter holidays were approaching and things were going well for Amber. The new saddle for Molly had arrived and she was going brilliantly in it. She'd had a few flatwork lessons with Caroline, and Molly moved so smoothly it was like gliding on a magic carpet. She'd even been persuaded by Jo to try some of their cross-country jumps with her. Amber had been reluctant at first, but Jo managed to coax her into it.

"Oh, I don't know. I haven't jumped her for ages. I'm not sure if Molly has even done any cross-country before..." Amber's confidence in the pony had been slowing unfolding like a delicate flower, but the flower, afraid of being crushed by a sudden rain shower, hadn't fully bloomed yet.

"I don't think she will have," Jo replied as she saddled Merry. Amber sat mounted on Molly in the yard, waiting for her. "The Drakes just did show jumping – outdoor in summer and indoor during winter. She's probably sick of the sight of show jumps. I bet she'd love cross-country: something new and exciting for her."

"Hmmm, yeah, great. Look what happened last time she did something new and exciting – she bolted." Molly's ears flicked back as Amber's voice rose in pitch.

"Yeah, but…" Jo led Merry out of the stable and vaulted straight on her, wriggling on her belly into the saddle before throwing her long right leg over and sitting upright. "You weren't expecting that then; you'd be ready for her now, and you're a much better rider now too, thanks to all you've done with Honey." Jo rode towards her jumping paddock, meaning that Amber had to follow, abandoning the hack she had planned. "Start with some of the show jumps and then, if you're happy, try some of the cross-country fences. Just see how it goes." Jo took charge, as usual.

Amber tensed and tightened her grip on the reins unconsciously. She wasn't wearing her body protector since she hadn't been expecting to jump, and she'd agreed with her parents that she'd build back up to jumping gradually. But they hadn't factored in the force that was Jo.

Jo shortened her stirrups and started warming up, so Amber felt obliged to do the same. At least no-one else was there watching. If it all went disastrously, no-one would know except Jo.

She started to trot Molly around the perimeter of the paddock but the pony was crab stepping sideways. Amber held her breath and went to tighten her hold on the reins again, until she remembered Caroline telling her that a tense rider makes a pony tense, especially a sensitive one like Molly. So, fighting her instinctive reactions, she let out her breath and her reins and put her leg on. As if to thank her for the freedom, Molly moved forward smoothly. Encouraged, Amber leaned forward fractionally and took her weight in her knees. She gave Molly a tiny signal to canter. Without the slightest fuss, Molly flowed into canter like a feather carried on a breeze. It felt so effortless yet powerful at the same time. Amber let out a small laugh. It was joy escaping from her like bubbles from a bottle of pop.

When she saw Jo starting to jump with Merry, excitement fizzed through her and she couldn't wait to try with Molly, her nerves temporarily held captive by happiness. Taking care to be more mindful of her riding and think about how her actions were interpreted by Molly, she presented her at a low straight-pole. It took all her will power to stop herself from grabbing the reins, but she was rewarded with a lovely jump from Molly. Amber patted her gratefully and continued around the field, taking the planks, parallel, blue barrels and the double with ease.

When she pulled up, patting Molly vigorously with delight, Jo grinned mischievously. "Wow, you could power a small country with that smile! Happy, I take it?"

Amber didn't reply; just carried on stroking Molly's neck lovingly.

"So…cross-country fences?" Jo looked hopeful.

Amber was so full of euphoria; her uncertainty had been squeezed out – there was no longer any room for it.

"Oh, go on then! She feigned reluctance, knowing Jo would be fully aware of her true feelings.

"Whoop whoop! Come on then. You can follow me if you want a lead."

***

That night, Amber could barely sleep. Even after a relaxing bath before bed, she was still alight with elation as she continued to re-live her afternoon. Jumping Jo's cross-country fences with Molly had blown Amber's mind. She already knew that cross-country was her favourite thing since she'd discovered it with Honey, but it felt even better on Molly. It seemed unlikely that Molly had ever done any cross-country before, but she'd loved it and jumped everything boldly. By the time she'd finished riding her, Amber had been filled with overwhelming love for her pony and never wanted to get off her.

Eventually, Jo had decided that the ponies had done enough and they'd ridden back into the yard. While Jo dismounted and led Merry into her stable, she said something that sent Amber into a spin.

She'd once again been patting Molly and convincing herself that what she'd just done was real and not a dream, when Jo's voice reached out of the stable and punctured her reverie.

"…Molly for the tetrathlon instead."

"What?" Amber called towards the stable where Merry's head was leaning over the door, but Jo was nowhere to be seen.

An arm appeared over the stable door and the bolt was slipped back to reveal Jo, laden with Merry's tack. As she flicked the kick bolt on with her foot and dumped the saddle on a stand next to the door, she repeated, "You should ride Molly in the tetrathlon instead of Honey. She'd be brilliant at it and would easily get round inside the time."

The balloon of happiness that enveloped Amber felt like it had been pricked by something sharp and started to deflate.

"Oh…I…" Amber stopped patting and tried to get her thoughts to stop playing leap-frog in her head. *Why do I suddenly feel cold?* she wondered. "Honey's gone clear around Brantfort's course – she even won there at the end of last year. She isn't the fastest but she's reliable. Molly might be awful at ditches or water for all we know."

"She goes through streams on hacks no bother and we could easily find some ditches on the fells to practise over. Brantfort is having a One Day Event on Easter Sunday. Why don't you take Molly? If you do the ninety class, it'll be the same course we'll be doing for the tetrathlon, so it'll be perfect practice."

"I'm already entered for that on Honey though."

"Yeah, but in the eighty, right? For the tetrathlon, our age group have to jump ninety centimetres. Can Honey manage a full course at that height? It'd be no problem to change your entry – just get your mum to ring their DC and ask if you can switch classes. They won't mind."

Amber rode back to the farm with her mind in turmoil. She was bursting to tell her parents about how brilliant Molly had been, but worried how they'd react, since she wasn't even meant to be jumping at all yet. And what would they say about taking Molly to a One Day Event so soon? Did she even want to take her? Yes, today had been brilliant, but was it tempting fate to go to a competition so soon? The course at Brantfort Bridge often caught out even experienced horses and she didn't want to create another disaster with Molly through impatience, just as things were starting to go well. Not to mention that it would feel disloyal to Honey to replace her after all she'd done to rebuild Amber's confidence after Molly demolished it. It would be like she was being relegated to 'second best pony' position again, despite never putting a foot wrong.

But this time, it wasn't just about her – there was the team to consider, and Honey's inevitable time faults could prove costly to her score, and therefore the team's score. Jo's words echoed in her mind, 'can Honey manage a full course at that height?' The truth was, she didn't know.

What should I do?

As she lay in bed that night, trying to get to sleep, a tug of war raged in her mind keeping her awake. Which pony should she choose?

- Sixteen -

Here We Come

As Amber got dressed and put her hair into a lopsided and lumpy French plait – *why can't I get it straight and without bumps like Jo?* – she rehearsed what she would say to her parents over breakfast. She still needed to tell them about jumping Molly yesterday, as she'd chickened out when she got back to the farm and said everything was fine when she was asked how her ride had been. And she also needed to tell them that she wanted to substitute Honey for Molly in the One Day Event. She had made up her mind after a sleepless night.

Her thoughts had gone round and round like a roulette wheel before finally coming to rest on the idea that she had nothing to lose by taking Molly to the One Day Event. If it went badly, then at least she'd know not to take Molly as her mount for the tetrathlon. And if it turned out that Molly didn't like the big ditch or the manky water jump, both of those fences had alternatives she could take. It would mean picking up fifteen penalties but should prevent elimination.

There was also the thought nagging in the back of her mind that all her friends would be on their competition ponies. Jo on the perfect Merry, Chelsea on Skylark – who could be a bit temperamental but was brilliant on a good day. Even Emily on Pink, who she knew through messages with Emily had been a bit difficult since they'd got her. The pony had been reasonably priced because, although she was a capable jumper, she'd terrified her previous child owner by repeatedly taking off with her. Emily said she'd been trying to do it with her too, and their relationship was a battle of wills at the moment. In typical Emily style, though, she wasn't getting stressed over it. She was getting on with it and trying to find the best way to work with the flighty mare.

And then of course, there was Natalie, still tearing around the show jumping circuit with Rocky, picking up prizes wherever they went. Instagram was constantly filled with pictures of her and Elisha Templeton and their stash of red rosettes. Amber didn't want to be left behind or to have people talking about her. She could imagine some of the comments. *'There's that Amber Anderson. She's got Frankie Drake's wonderful pony, Just Molly, but she's always on that Fell pony. Such a waste. Someone else could have had a great pony there.'*

Amber let out a deep breath as she left her bedroom and went downstairs. She would need to be convincing to get her parents on side. If they detected any trace of doubt in her, they'd say she had to stick with Honey and there would be nothing she could do to change their minds. At least, she remembered, her dad was at work today so she only had to deal with one rather than both of them together.

When she arrived in the kitchen, Mrs Anderson was eating toast whilst reading her current book. Stig the cat was trying hard to sit on it to force her to give him some attention, but she gently and repeatedly fended him off. Amber poured herself a bowl of muesli, added some milk and sat down at the table. Stig turned his attention to her and padded over on the table top to stare at her cereal bowl. He knew that when she was finished, he'd be allowed to drink the milk that was left over.

"Mum," Amber started, spooning muesli into her mouth while the cat watched every mouthful.

"Mmmm," she replied, distracted by the events taking place on the page before her.

"Um, well, yesterday when I was at Jo's, we didn't actually go for a ride out." She waited for a response but got none so she carried on. "We did some jumping in her paddock instead and Molly was really good and we even did some cross-country fences and I want to take her to the One Day Event instead of Honey so can you ring up and change the entry?" She blurted it all out in one breath with no full stops, to get it over with, then shoved another mouthful of muesli towards her face while she waited for her mother's reaction.

Mrs Anderson didn't react. She kept reading without looking up and Amber debated whether she should say it all again, wondering if she'd even heard her. She could get so engrossed in books; the rest of the world was blocked out completely. But then her mother closed her book and pushed it slowly away from her, fixing her blue-eyed gaze on Amber.

"What?" she said simply.

Amber tried to read her face to see if she was angry but she couldn't tell. Tentatively, she said it all again.

Mrs Anderson stared at her daughter across the table and Amber stared at her mother's chin, not quite able to hold her eye contact. Stig took advantage of the distraction to start lapping milk from the unfinished bowl of muesli.

Eventually, she spoke. "I don't think that's a good idea, love. I'm glad things are going well but I don't think you should rush it. Work with Molly at home for now and use Honey for competitions. This wasn't Jo's idea, was it?" she asked shrewdly.

"No, it's my idea." Amber knew it would seem better if it was what she wanted.

"Please, Mum, let's just try. If it doesn't go well, *then* I can go back to working her at home, but it might be fine. It probably will be fine."

Again, her mother regarded her. It was unlike Amber not to accept 'no' when she was told. Her daughter seemed different somehow lately. She wasn't a little girl anymore and was starting to come out of her shell. Mrs Anderson sighed as she realised their relationship was changing. They were going to need to compromise more now that she was growing up, rather than just telling her what she had to do. *Why is she so determined to ride Molly in a competition so soon?* Mrs Anderson wondered. The pony had done nothing but terrify her since they'd got her. They'd actually been thinking of selling her now that Amber had Honey to compete and have a good time on. She didn't want to see her daughter get hurt or frightened again, but Amber seemed intent on trying to start afresh with the pony, and she admired her resilience.

"I'll tell you what we'll do." She sighed again. "You're having a lesson with Caroline today. I'll ask her to do some jumping with you instead of flatwork and I'll watch. Then I'll have a chat with Caroline and when your dad comes home from work later, we'll discuss it. It's not a no, it's a maybe."

"Okay," Amber agreed, pushing the cat out of her breakfast and placing him on the floor so that her mum couldn't see her face. She didn't know whether she was pleased or not that it 'wasn't a no' and she worried her indecision would show. Amber wasn't very good at hiding her feelings. She would just have to keep acting like this was what she wanted while she figured it out for herself.

***

Caroline was soon persuaded when Mrs Anderson explained the situation and asked her to give Amber a jumping lesson. Wearing her body protector this time, Amber warmed up and popped a few small fences before they were raised. Molly flowed over everything like silk and Caroline complimented Amber's riding, much to her delight as she so wanted to impress her quiet and patient instructor.

"There's not much we can do to practise cross-country in here, since we've only got show jumps, but I've got an idea. Hang on." She went through the gate and disappeared into the farmyard.

Amber walked Molly around the small paddock on a loose rein until Caroline returned with the black plastic wrapping from a big bale of hay which she had brought to represent a ditch. She laid it on the ground and Mrs Anderson helped her to smooth it out and fold it to a width of around two feet. They then put a couple of poles on the long edges to hold it down and stop it flapping.

"We don't know if she's ever jumped any ditches before, so before she's asked to take on the real thing, let's try this. Get her trotting and ride her positively up to it, see if she'll pop over it. Don't look down, keep your head up and be prepared in case she gives a bigger jump than needed."

Driving Molly into an active trot, Amber turned her towards the improvised ditch. She rode as instructed but as Molly got to the point of take-off, she slammed on the brakes and snorted at the black plastic. She tried to dodge around it but Amber was quick enough to hold her in place and get her to halt. "It's alright, lass, it's just a bit of plastic," she reassured the pony, stroking her neck to soothe her. "Just have a look at it. There's nothing to be scared of."

"Erm, Amber?"

Amber looked up as Caroline stepped shyly forward. She recognised that Caroline was about to 'tell her off' about something. Whereas many instructors would yell at you if you did something wrong, and forcefully tell you what you should be doing, Caroline always delivered criticism flinchingly, as if it hurt her to do so.

"Err, don't stroke or pat her when she's done something wrong. I know you're trying to reassure her, but you're sending mixed messages." Caroline stepped close so that Amber could hear her softly spoken advice. "We pat horses to reward them and tell them when we're happy with them. If you pat her when she's refused to do what you've asked, she will think she was right not to trust you and to stop and look, rather than jumping on the first attempt. If she refuses, you just sit quietly, let her look, then re-present her positively. If she jumps it *then* give her a big pat. She needs to learn to trust you and do what you ask without question. For her to do that, you need to be consistent so that you don't confuse her. Now she's had a look at it, come again and ride positively with lots of leg."

Amber steered Molly away feeling totally stupid. Caroline's words made perfect sense. *Why have I never thought of that?* She'd often seen other riders patting their horses when they were nervous or spooked, but she could see now how that must be confusing for the horse. She'd been so focused on the issue of building *her* trust in Molly, she hadn't even considered that it needed to work both ways: Molly needed to trust her too.

Frustrated with herself, she gave Molly a positive nudge with her legs and urged her towards the ditch. This time Molly tried to veer to the right but Amber quickly straightened her. Molly then tried to go left, but again found that her rider wasn't going to allow that option. "Go on girl!" Amber kicked on and allowed her hands to go forwards in anticipation of the jump. Molly hesitated then made an overly large, rather crooked jump over the scary black bag, but was rewarded with lots of pats and praise. Amber repeated the ditch several more times, including from the other direction, until Molly was jumping it calmly and smoothly.

Caroline gave Molly a gentle pat at the end of the lesson and congratulated Amber. "That was great," she said, pushing her wavy brown hair out of her face. "You're ready to try the real thing now. There are some decent ditches you could try on the fells but take care not to pick one where the take-off and landing are boggy. Make sure you find one in some firm ground."

"Oh, I will, thank you. That was brilliant."

As usual, Caroline blushed at the praise.

On the way home in the car, Amber asked her mother what she thought of her and Molly's jumping.

"Yes, I was pleasantly surprised. You and Molly seem to have gelled much more now, and you're riding with more confidence too. It was good to watch." Mrs Anderson had to keep her eyes on the road, but she flashed a quick smile at her daughter.

"So…can I take her to the One Day Event then?" Amber asked hopefully. She was now feeling more certain that it was what she wanted.

"Hmmm, we'll see. Like I said, I'll discuss it with your dad."

Amber smiled to herself as she slipped into a daydream of riding Molly round a Badminton sized cross-country course while people watched and cheered, gasping in amazement at their bravery and skill. *Watch out everyone, here we come*, she thought.

– Seventeen –

Ready or Not

At last, the Easter holiday came around. Amber spent the first week doing more jumping on Molly so that her dad could observe their progress. He was particularly resistant to the idea of taking Molly to the One Day Event in Honey's place. She had tried to persuade him but he looked uncomfortable whenever it was brought up and said that she'd be better off sticking with Honey. Amber couldn't work out why he was so against the idea until she arrived at the conclusion that he must think she wasn't capable. The thought stung her and strengthened her determination to prove herself. Unusually for her, she'd insisted on him watching her jumping with Molly in Caroline's paddock. He had to admit that he was impressed with their progress but still seemed reluctant.

"It's one thing to jump well in here – it's just a small space – but a wide-open cross-country course is a different thing altogether. I just don't..." he trailed off. Mr Anderson held himself responsible for Amber's recent accidents and he didn't want the responsibility of giving the go-ahead for this latest idea, in case it ended badly. He didn't want to disappoint Amber or burst her bubble of happiness, but he knew he'd feel better if she stuck to safe, reliable Honey and ignored the urge to match her friends and their ponies. It was true that this was part of Amber's drive but he had no idea that a desire to impress him was also fuelling Amber's ambitions with Molly.

"Well...I know!" Amber had declared. "Let's go up on the fells and try some ditch jumping. If we all go, you can see for yourself and if she behaves and jumps the ditches...?"

And so, on the Wednesday before Easter Sunday, the whole Anderson family headed up towards the appropriately named Cold Fell where the winds blew strongly enough to knock you sideways. They had been up there on several rides with the riding school and since buying the Fell ponies, but never with Molly. The Fellies were able to canter along, sure and nimble-footed as they

137

negotiated the undulations of the land they were bred to navigate, but nobody knew how Molly would react to the wildness of a landscape she had never encountered.

They started with a smart trot along the road from the end of the farm track to the gate which took them onto the fell. They then allowed the ponies to walk, three abreast to give Molly time to accustom herself to the springiness of the mossy ground and find her way through the bracken. They steered clear of areas they knew to be full of rabbit holes or ground unsuitable for the ponies, until they came to a stretch that was open and crying out to be cantered upon. The Fell ponies, long used to this being a canter place, started to walk faster and toss their heads, their long black manes rippling in the wind. Even Pearl was keen to get going.

"Okay?" Mr Anderson asked Amber as they prepared to canter. Amber nodded. Knowing what this ride was going to entail, she'd shortened her stirrups from her normal hacking length, as shorter stirrups made her feel stronger and more secure. She prayed that her fragile faith in Molly would pay off.

The three ponies set off together like a cavalry charge, the bright chestnut of Molly's coat flanked by the

Fell ponies like two black bookends. Their hooves pounded in rhythmic unison as they matched strides. Molly leaned on her bit; she would have liked to lengthen and increase the pace but she allowed Amber to hold her in a steady canter. Glorying in the power she could feel at her fingertips and the bunched muscles beneath her, Amber loosened her hold on the reins slightly. Molly reacted instantly and her speed increased, but Amber still felt in control. Her eyes blurred with tears from the cold air and the landscape ahead of her became a kaleidoscope of mauve, marmalade and moss colours. By the time she pulled Molly up, her parents were well behind them, trotting to catch up.

"Are you okay?" Her mother's shrill voice reached her faintly as the wind caught it and hurled it into the distance.

"Yes!" Amber laughed, "That was brilliant!" Molly still felt alarming compared to the Fell ponies; there was so much potential for what she *could* do, but now it seemed more exhilarating than frightening.

Before they entered a gate into the forestry to return to the farm, they found a broad ditch and played at jumping it for several minutes. Mr Anderson took the lead on Honey, with Molly happily following. Even Mrs Anderson had a go on Pearl. Amber finished off with a couple of turns without taking a lead from Honey to ensure that Molly would jump the ditch without a pony in front of her to follow, then they headed into the forestry and back to the farm.

"She was so good, wasn't she?" Amber was jubilant for the duration of the ride home and chattered non-stop, reliving the thrilling experience on the fell.

"So, can I take her at the weekend?"

**

On Easter Sunday, the Andersons pulled onto the field at Brantfort Bridge and lowered the front ramp of their trailer to reveal a chestnut face. Mr Anderson had eventually given his blessing for Molly to take Honey's place as a trial and had phoned Brantfort Pony Club's DC to ask for the entry to be changed. Amber had spent the last few days practising her dressage test. At swimming on Friday, she'd found out that Emily and Chelsea were also entered, and she already knew that Jo was going too. It was a strange feeling to know that they'd soon be competing together as a team, but at this event, they were individuals competing against each other.

Amber had been pleased when she'd learned it was all sorted and she could take Molly on Sunday. She'd spent her evenings since then watching her favourite event riders on YouTube. Her special favourite was an Irish rider called Amanda McCarthy who rode a chestnut that looked just like Molly. His name was Zero Fox and he was a gelding rather than a mare, but with his white socks and white blaze, he was like Molly's twin. He was described by one commentator as 'a vibrant ride'. At under 16hh, he was practically a pony competing at 5* level, but he bounced around the enormous courses, making the fences look easy. Amber watched them over and over again imagining that they were her and Molly. She couldn't wait for her chance to emulate them.

But now it was the day of the competition, all her hopes were crushed by nerves which had returned with a vengeance. It hadn't helped that they'd got to the venue early, so she'd have time to walk the cross-country course before she began, to find that the ninety track looked *enormous*, particularly one new, or rather, updated fence. This fence had been an old, ramshackle wall; the remains of a dry-stone wall that had disintegrated over time. But the wall had been repaired and added to, so that there were now three different height options. It was both higher and wider than it had been before – even the lowest element - and was now topped with a railway sleeper. Its square solidity was intimidating. Amber stared incredulously at the fence, trying to ignore the panicked voice in her head telling her that it would be scary enough on Honey, but Molly had had a bad experience with a wall in the past and was likely to take exception to this monstrosity. The ditch also appeared deeper and wider than usual and the water jump looked and smelled like the contents of a witch's cauldron.

By the time she'd got to the end of the cross-country course and started to head back to the parking area, her legs felt like they didn't belong to her and she had to stop and rest against a gnarly old oak tree, taking deep breaths to try and quell the nausea. A knobbly piece of bark dug into her back painfully, and she concentrated on the discomfort as a distraction.

See, you should have brought Honey, her inner voice pointed out unhelpfully. Amber contemplated hiding behind the tree all day. Everyone was here. All her friends, her parents, people who knew Molly. The thought of failing in front of them all was paralysing. She

142

squeezed her eyes tight and fought back an overwhelming urge to cry. She had to pull herself together or she'd have failed before she even tried.

Come on, you need to move, she told herself. The trouble was, her feet wouldn't listen to her brain, and she remained stuck to the tree as if she was its prisoner.

- Eighteen -

Mistake

Amber eventually managed to remove herself from the grip of the oak tree and trudged back to the trailer park. Her stomach, which felt like a nest of snakes, coiled even further the moment she saw her mother. She was holding a tacked-up Molly, craning her neck to scan the area around her like a periscope. Her blue eyes were twin searchlights both ready to lock on to their target when they found it: Amber.

Amber slid behind the nearest trailer to hide and received an inquisitive nudge from a small bay pony who had been tied there without a haynet to occupy him. It hadn't been a particularly strong shove, not like one of Pearl's battering ram head butts, but Amber felt so weak, she staggered and almost fell. Losing the cover of the trailer, she spied her mother again, her face set like a hard, marble statue, her eyebrows a V of annoyance. When her combing eyes found Amber, she experienced the Medusa effect of her mother's anger aimed at her and turned to stone.

"Amber! Where have you been? Get over here *now*."

Molly, looking exactly like a miniature Zero Fox, had been dozing. She'd been to so many competitions in her life, she paid no attention to the frenzied atmosphere of people and horses rushing about her. But Mrs Anderson's screech right in her ear startled and unsettled her. She shook her head roughly in annoyance so that several of her plaits came loose. Amber, with the threatening taste of vomit creeping into the back of her throat, was reeled towards them by the force of her mother's gaze.

"*Where* have you been?" she snapped again, not waiting for an answer. "You've been ages. Your test is in five minutes and you're not even ready to get on! Hurry up."

With fingers that suddenly felt as fat and useless as sausages, Amber fumbled to peel off her hoody and tracky bottoms. Luckily, she already had her jodhs, shirt and tie on underneath so she just needed to change her boots, shrug on her jacket, persuade her uncooperative hair into a hairnet and cram her hat on her head.

Just as her mother was legging her up onto Molly, a flustered Mr Anderson appeared. He had clearly been looking for her as relief smoothed his features when he saw her.

"Ah, phew." He glanced up at Amber's face and noted that it was the same shade of white as her brand-new dressage gloves. "You er, won't have long to warm up but I've asked the steward if you can go at the end of the class and they're happy to move you to the end, since there are other riders there ready to go. Okay?"

Amber nodded silently, not trusting herself to open her mouth. She waited for her mother to wrestle Molly's last loose plait back into its band, "told her she should've stitched these in," being muttered under her breath. Then, without looking at her parents' faces, Amber pointed Molly in the direction of the dressage warm up area. It was on hilly ground, squeezed in beside the dressage arenas and the show jumping course, making it less than ideal for warming up for the test.

The furious whispers of her parents accompanied her as they followed behind. Fragments of their words buzzed around her head like poisonous wasps. "Terrified,"…"mistake,"… "not ready,"… "disaster."

She closed her eyes, breathed deeply and tried to run through the test in her head, but as soon as she recalled, *Enter in working trot and proceed down centre line without halting*, her parents' words started an invasion.

Mistake, terrified, disaster, not ready, terrified, disaster, not ready. Mistake, mistake, MISTAKE.

Molly felt like a plank of wood beneath her. All she'd learned from Caroline about softening her hands, keeping her leg on and allowing Molly to relax and move forward into a receptive contact had been buried by self-doubt. Everyone else warming up around her – the riders in the Open class – looked so professional and polished, she wondered what she was even doing there. *I should've stuck to hacking with Pearl*, she thought. *I can't do this.*

"Amber Anderson? You're next," a steward called and pointed towards the rider currently saluting at the end of their test. It was a sign for Amber to come over and start moving around the outside of the arena until the judge pipped the car horn to signal she should start her test.

"Earth calling Amber!" she heard as she rode towards the dressage arena the steward had pointed at. Somehow, she'd failed to notice that the rider finishing their test was Emily. Her friend was riding out past her, patting Pink. The pony's arched neck, topped with her black Mohican mane, gave her a striking resemblance to the Trojan horse.

"I said good luck, you zombie!"

Still unable to get her brain to formulate a reply, she nodded once more and rode on, frantically trying to recall the movements of the test.

HONK! The car parked at C, containing the dressage judge and her writer, gave a short, sharp signal that she should begin.

Right, come on. We can do this, she told herself firmly. *But not if I ride like a potato.*

As she rounded the turn to enter the arena at A and trot up the centre line, Amber finally forced herself to over-rule her fear and ride as she knew she must. She tried her absolute best to relax, to use her aids softly and to respond quickly to Molly's reactions. The pony was unsettled at first by the sudden change in her rider, who had been as rigid as an iron pole only a moment before, and the first part of the test was jagged and awkward. By the time they'd changed on to the right rein, however, Molly's trot had settled into an even and regular rhythm and her final canter was as silky as ever. She trotted as straight as an arrow up the centre line and her halt was smooth and square. A smile broke through and Amber patted her pony gratefully.

"Good girl." Although the test had started badly, she was sure they'd be awarded some decent scores for the second half. They'd done it. The first phase was complete, she hadn't forgotten the test or made any mistakes and Molly had responded so well when she'd finally started to ride properly. Her grin widened as she reflected on the best parts of the test while riding out of the arena on a long rein towards her parents.

"Well done, that looked great!" Mr Anderson gave her a one-man round of applause.

"Yes, well done love." Her mother patted her on the leg. "You did so well. We could see how nervous you were before you started and we weren't expecting it to go so well. Terrific!"

Amber sat up tall and absorbed the praise until she almost floated out of the saddle. But just as she was beginning to feel as buoyant as a feather, the anchor returned to pin her to the ground when Mr Anderson said, "But you're late for the cross-country now. We'll just have to stick some boots on Molly, you put your cross-country top on over your shirt and throw your body protector on. Let's hope you're in time before they start changing the flags for the Open class."

- Nineteen -

Out of Time

At most One Day Events, the show jumping follows the dressage with the cross-country being the last of the three phases to complete. But, at Brantfort Bridge, with the dressage warmup being right next to the show jumping course, they ran the cross-country second so that those still doing their dressage weren't put off by horses and ponies jumping right beside them.

With three of them involved, it was a quick turnaround to complete the transformation from dressage participants into a cross-country team. Mrs Anderson worked with surprising dexterity to remove Molly's plaits at Amber's insistence.

"We haven't got time to take plaits out. You're already late for the time you were given to ride. Just leave them in," she'd argued.

"No, I want them out. I...I don't feel right when I see all that long neck stretched out in front of me with no mane to grab hold of," Amber replied, thinking of Honey's lovely long mane. "Take them out...please."

And so, while Mrs Anderson raked her fingers through the plaits, pulling out bands and loosening Molly's now curly mane, Mr Anderson quickly secured brushing and over-reach boots to Molly's legs and front feet. Amber did as instructed, and threw her riding jacket hurriedly onto the back seat of the car, replacing it with her green and navy blue quartered rugby top. She didn't have time to change the silk on her riding hat, so the blue velvet cover from the dressage phase remained. She mounted quickly and hiked her stirrups up several holes. Just as she thought she was ready to head down the road to the cross-country start, she realised she'd forgotten to put her number bib back on so she had to dismount and wriggle her way into it.

When she eventually arrived in the collecting ring, the steward checked her over to ensure she was safe and legal, and told her she was next to go. Amber barely had time to notice Emily leaving the starting box on Pink when she was told she had two minutes until her turn.

"But…I've just got here. I haven't jumped a practice fence yet!" Her voice rose in panic.

"Sorry love, but you're the last to go in this class. Got to get it finished for the next lot to start on time. We can't wait for you. Just go and jump a fence now." The steward informed her regretfully.

When her parents arrived to watch her, she'd had just one pop over a practice fence before being called over by the starter.

"Good luck!" Mr Anderson waved, feeling his heart hit the floor. This was the phase he was most worried about. While he knew that he could trust Honey to look after Amber on a cross-country course, this was probably Molly's first attempt. Who knew how she'd handle it? He wanted to tell Amber that they'd be watching from the top of the hill but he didn't get the chance as she was being counted down from ten.

"Four…three…two…one…go, and good luck!" The starter called, pressing the button on his stopwatch.

Amber was scarcely able to register what was happening before they took off. Last summer she'd taken Honey on her first cross-country attempt at Pony Club camp, and she'd felt sick with nerves then too. But this was even worse. It was the biggest course she'd ever tackled, and it was on Molly, who had the potential to completely run away with her if she chose to; she'd done it before. Or perhaps she'd behave herself but get eliminated, something that Honey had never done. The shame of failure on this pony would be a hundred times worse than on Honey as no-one ever expected anything of her since she was 'just a Fell pony'.

As she rode out of the start box, Amber knew it didn't matter what breed of pony Molly was or how good a show jumper she was. She'd never done this before and she needed her rider to give her confidence. Amber had learned to her cost before that there was never any time when you could take a pony for granted and just be a passenger. She needed to ride this course all the way around and leave nothing to chance. She visualised herself as Amanda McCarthy with the pocket rocket, Zero Fox, beneath her and pushed for the first fence.

Fence one was a straightforward brush fence which Molly neatly hopped over, but fence two, named The Monkey Puzzle fence due to the huge monkey puzzle tree that grew beside it, was a solid box with ground that sloped away on the landing side. Amber rode Molly strongly at it and the pony responded, jumping with more vigour than the fence needed. Due to the sloping ground on the landing side, Molly's large jump pitched Amber onto her neck. Sitting up quickly, she steadied the pony and approached fence three – a downhill double – from a trot. Molly jumped this fence more economically, meaning they landed over the second part in good balance. They cantered into the wood to take on the first of two large logs – left over from storm fallen trees – which Molly soared over.

"Okay girl, that's good. Now for the steps." Amber knew it was unlikely that Molly had ever seen a row of steps before, so she collected her into a bouncy canter to ensure she had the necessary energy for the uphill staircase carved into the side of a woodland bank. Molly understood and powered up the three steps enthusiastically. She had never done anything like this before and was electrified with adrenalin. She leaned on

155

the bit as they cantered up the hill, out of the wood, but Amber checked her and she listened, wondering where they were going next.

The first fence out of the wood was a tyre jump which Molly had a look at and jumped cautiously before they took the log pile and chair near the church. Then it was on to the ditch and rails: this course's bogey fence for so many. Amber knew this was where her parents would be to watch as it was the highest point of the course and most of the rest of the fences could be seen from there.

She checked Molly and brought her back to a trot to get her straight for the first set of rails. Then, with a gentle aid, she nudged her into a collected canter. Molly obliged immediately and jumped the first rail sweetly, but when she landed and saw the huge black ditch ahead of her, she baulked and tried to swerve away. Amber was ready for her and kept her straight. Molly slowed almost to a stop, her long neck disappearing in front of Amber as she tried to take in what was ahead of her. Resisting the desire to let her look at the ditch with a pat of reassurance, Amber recalled Caroline's words; *Don't reward her for doing the wrong thing. She needs to trust you and do what you ask. Only pat her when she's done the right thing*, and dug her heels into Molly's sides. "Go on!" she urged.

Molly stopped at the edge of the ditch and teetered there for a moment; her brain filled with indecision. But with Amber's constant urging, she bunched herself up and launched over the ditch from a standstill. The landing jolted Amber and she lost her balance, but somehow they managed to scramble over the second rail and were on their way. Amber took a second to pull Molly back and straighten herself up before they were off again. They were only halfway around the course but Amber was ecstatic.

"Yes! Good girl! Come on!" She clicked her tongue and Molly surged forward. Honey would have been getting tired by now and Amber would need to nurse her home, but Molly was just warming-up. It felt like they already had a clear round. Molly, sensing her rider's new enthusiasm, flew over the ski jump, the skinny log, the palisade, gate, and zigzag fence until they were approaching the dreaded wall.

Amber knew she needed to approach the wide, solid fence with an open, positive stride, but her fear of the wall paralysed her and she felt some other force take over as if she were just a puppet. She felt herself slow Molly down, back to a show jumping canter and screamed at herself, *No, what are you doing? Don't slow down. Push on. She needs more impulsion for this fence*. But the invisible puppet-master continued to steady the pony until Molly reached the point of take-off with no impetus whatsoever. Most ponies, finding themselves with no stride for take-off and no impulsion to carry them over the fence, would have ground to a halt in front of it or ducked out, but Molly was enjoying herself and her blood was up. It wasn't pretty to look at, but somehow the pony managed to tuck her legs up and twist her body, so that, awkward and uncomfortable as it was, they managed to clear the huge wall.

"Yes!" Amber punched the air with her whip and patted Molly wildly. There were only three fences left. Was she actually going to achieve a clear round? She didn't dare believe it.

She turned Molly to head towards fence seventeen, an upright of railway sleepers on a downhill slope, and gasped. As she came over the brow of the hill, Emily was just ahead of her: a vision in pink, wearing hot pink colours on her pink pony. She was approaching the fence

Amber was aiming for. How could she have caught Emily up?

As Emily cleared the sleepers and turned left towards the penultimate fence – the water jump – Molly's ears pricked as she noticed the pony in front of her. Her competitive instinct kicked in and she flew down the hill and cleared the sleepers faster than Amber wanted. "Woah, steady girl!" Amber shortened her reins and tried to steady Molly as she lined her up for the water jump. But Molly's attention was focused on the pony ahead of her, not her rider. Amber tried to hold Molly back to give Emily time to drop into the water, and pass through it to the other side, but Molly did not want to listen. She fought against her rider and snatched the bit in her teeth. Just as Pink was jumping out and heading to the Irish bank, the last fence on the course, Molly hurtled after her.

With all her attention directed at the pony she wanted to catch, Molly ignored Amber's aids to anchor her and misjudged the obstacle in front of her. Instead of slowing to drop down into the sludgy water and crossing through, Molly raced at it and tried to jump the entire thing in one move. Amber gasped as she felt the pony extend, reaching for the other side. There was a moment, like one in a comical cartoon, where they hung, suspended above the gloop beneath them before they were falling, falling.

If Molly had been moving more slowly, she might have been able to keep her feet, but her forward momentum, combined with the thick, gluey contents of the water jump, meant that the outcome was inevitable. She'd cleared well over half the distance of the water crossing, but with a couple of metres between her and dry land, Amber felt Molly's knees buckle under her. Her head went down and her body tipped sideways, spilling Amber into the foul, stinking gunge.

- Twenty -

Grounded

Although Molly had somehow managed to keep herself upright and avoid falling in the water, Amber was not so lucky. After sliding around in the gunge for a minute she was able to get to her feet and stand up, resembling a hippopotamus after a mud bath. She was covered in sludge and slimy pondweed and was soaked through.

The fence judges, having recovered from the shock, and mopped up the tea they'd spilt on themselves, sprung into action. One of them reached tentatively for Molly's dangling reins and coaxed her out onto dry land while the other took charge of Amber.

"There we are dear, reach for me, that's it." Amber managed to take the lady's hand but it looked more likely that she was going to pull her helper into the water as she was literally stuck in the mud.

Her parents soon arrived, having run frantically down the hill when they'd seen their daughter disappear from Molly's back. With each of them taking an arm, they managed to drag Amber onto the bank beside the water. Both were relieved she was unharmed by the experience but neither could help wrinkling their noses. Amber stank as she stood between them, dripping.

"Well, that was exciting," the fence judge holding Molly exclaimed. Mrs Anderson rushed over to take Molly from her. She was one of those pristine women with perfect hair and makeup, manicured nails and an outfit that looked like she'd stepped out of a country life magazine. Mrs Anderson was terrified that the pony might soon shake herself like a dog and spray this perfect woman with all the mud and algae tangled in her tail.

"Yes, it was like being at Burghley when Princess Anne came off at the Trout Hatchery. That was dreadfully muddy too!" The other judge, an older but equally well-dressed woman, was inappropriately delighted at Amber's predicament. Seeming to become aware of this as she watched the young girl begin to shiver in her soaking jodhpurs, the woman added, "I know this wasn't what you'd have been hoping for dear, but it makes you a proper rider now. It even happens to the professionals, so you mustn't worry. At least you're both alright."

Just then, the paramedic pulled up, right in time to cut off any other infuriating remarks. He quickly assessed Amber and passed her fit to ride if she wished to carry on.

"It seems a shame not to when you've only got one fence left, but, well…I think everyone would understand if you decided not to bother." He winked sympathetically.

It was a tough choice. She could either get back on Molly and complete the course but get her lovely new saddle all wet or she could walk all the way back to the trailer in her sodden clothes and boots. Her mind was made up when a man zoomed up on a quad bike to alter the flags on the water jump to make it ready for the final class which was waiting to start.

"You finishing or retiring, love?" he asked, "'cos I've got to get this last fence flagged for the next class."

Quickly making her decision, Amber walked awkwardly over to Molly, her feet squelching in her boots. She gathered up her reins and bent her left leg at the knee to signal that she wanted a leg up. Water trickled out of her boot. Mrs Anderson's eyes widened in surprise but she quickly obliged and hoisted Amber back into the saddle. Squirming at the discomfort of her soggy bottom, she turned Molly in the direction of the finish and was quickly on and off the Irish bank and through the finish flags to complete the course. She found that Emily was still there, waiting for her.

"OMG. You legend! Look at you." She suppressed a smile. "I thought I'd had a bad round but…" she trailed off, shaking her head. The girls set off back up the track towards the trailers, riding side by side. Pink had her top lip curled up revealing her teeth. It looked like she was smiling, but as her mouth was strapped shut by a very tight flash noseband, Amber guessed that she was desperate to be able to open and stretch her mouth and breathe properly.

"Wh…what happened to you?" Amber asked, her teeth starting to chatter.

"Oh, it was fine really, but two stops at the ditch. I could have jumped the alternative but I wanted to make sure she'd jumped the ditch so that she'll hopefully go over it at the tetrathlon. But what about you? How on earth did you end up in the water jump?"

Amber explained how Molly had locked on to Pink and been so determined to catch her, she'd tried to jump over the whole thing.

"You're joking? I'm so sorry. When I realised you'd caught me up, I was chuffed as I knew it meant you must be clear. And I thought it was probably a good thing – if Molly was in any doubt about going into that disgusting water, she'd use Pink as a lead and follow." Emily looked genuinely stricken. "But it's because of me you didn't get a clear!"

"No, it's not your fault. It's this *stupid* pony's."

Emily's head snapped around in shock at Amber's words.

"Stupid? Amber, I know coming off in the water wasn't part of the plan, but surely you're pleased with her? It was her first go at cross-country and if it hadn't been for me, she'd have gone clear." She continued staring at Amber, who had her eyes fixed on the ground. "She jumped the steps and the awful ditch and that new wall – did you see it? It's enormous now!"

Amber didn't reply. She was concentrating on holding in the sob that was threatening to escape, and it was burning her throat.

"Look, I know you're disappointed now but we'll look back at this in the future and laugh our heads off. It'll be a brilliant story to tell people…" Emily trailed off, not knowing what else to say as she saw a tear roll down Amber's cheek and drip off her chin. They rode through the gate into the trailer park in silence.

"Er, I need to get ready for the show jumping. See you later?"

Amber nodded and rode away.

Back at her own trailer, she slithered soggily from the saddle and was immediately enveloped in a fierce hug. Mrs Anderson pulled her close and fought the tears that were stinging her own eyes.

"I'm so sorry, doll. You were fantastic. You didn't deserve to have that happen."

Amber's reply was muffled against her mother's chest.

"Sorry, what?" She released her hold slightly and looked down at her daughter.

"I'm so useless!" Amber sobbed.

166

"What? Of course you're not useless. What a silly thing to say."

"I am." Amber dragged the back of a wet, muddy glove across her eyes, making her face even wetter. "That was a disaster. I can't ride Molly. I'm not good enough for her. She'd be better off with someone else. Someone who's not crap like me."

Mrs Anderson looked despairingly at her husband, stood holding Molly beside her.

"You are not crap." He said firmly, reaching out and putting a hand on Amber's shoulder. "You're just learning how to do all this and it's not easy. It's been hard for you, getting going with Molly, but she's had problems that have been nothing to do with you and more to do with a huge change in routine and a saddle that clearly didn't fit her. She's frightened you and we thought we'd be better off selling her and letting you stick with Honey, but you've kept on trying. You've listened and learned and worked so hard with her. We're so proud of your determination, Amber. We know you've been terrified, but you haven't given up."

He took his hand off Amber's shoulder and ran it over his greying hair. "But you don't need to be constantly fighting and feeling scared. If you want to sell Molly and go back to Honey, and even go back to just hacking out, that's fine. You don't need to do all this for our benefit. It's supposed to be fun."

Amber let his words sink in. They *were* proud of her. Despite the fact that she was standing there soaking wet and stinking, they were proud of her. She looked at Molly and realised that Emily was right. Just a few months ago, the idea of doing cross-country on Molly had seemed impossible, but now, here they were. And apart from a freak incident, the pony hadn't put a foot wrong. She'd even helped Amber out when she'd ridden badly at the wall. Amber reached out and stroked Molly's blaze. The idea of selling her or giving up was out of the question.

"Amber!" Jo was running towards her, looking odd in her riding jacket, shirt and tie and hat, combined with pyjama bottoms and jodhpur boots. "Emily told me what happened. I've just finished my show jumping, so you can borrow my jodhpurs. They're dry." She held them out, earnestly, waiting for Amber to take them. There was no 'if you're doing the show jumping,' from Jo. Even as Amber paused, Jo continued holding the jodhpurs out to her, fully expecting Amber to carry on and complete the competition.

Slowly, Amber reached out and took Jo's offering. "Thanks." She smiled, then laughed at her friend's appearance and pictured her attending the prize-giving dressed as she was now. She quickly dived into the trailer and changed. It was difficult to get the new jodhs on as her legs were damp and clammy. It was like trying to get changed after swimming, but she managed to wriggle her way into them. They were a bit long but she turned the bottoms up. Her socks were still soaking and she had to put her wet boots back on, but at least she was now partly dry.

Her body protector had kept most of her upper half dry so by the time she got back into her riding jacket, she looked much less like a swamp creature. She pulled her hoody out of the car and used it to wipe her saddle dry.

"Right," she said to Jo and her parents. "I've got a round of show jumping to do. Let's go."

– Twenty-One –

Snakes and Ladders

Now that she had nothing to lose, Amber could relax. The sixty-five penalties she'd picked up from her fall on the cross-country meant she was out of the running for a place and this gave her the freedom to ride like she was in the paddock at home. Gone was the robotic Amber of the morning. She had wet knickers, soggy socks and had made local Pony Club history by being the only rider who had ever landed in the water jump here – the most disgusting water jump anyone had ever seen. She had nothing to lose. And so, when her number was called and she rode into the show jumping arena, she could truly imagine herself as a top eventer, triumphing in the face of adversity. If it was good enough for Princess Anne, it was good enough for her.

She knew that Chelsea and Emily had managed to show jump clear, and even Jo had only picked up four faults on the notoriously careless Merry, but rather than being intimidated by the fact, she was inspired by it. Although the tetrathlon, their team event, didn't feature show jumping, it would still help to make them feel like a united team if they could all do well in one phase today.

The whistle blew and Molly reacted without needing a signal from Amber. She knew what it meant and wanted to get started. The pony had gotten bored with constant show jumping year after year, summer and winter with no rest, but she'd found her recent break from work even duller. Now, combined with a comfortable saddle that didn't nip her when she lifted her shoulders, and the introduction of a new activity into her life, she felt invigorated. The cross-country made her feel alive and free and she was starting to get used to this new rider. This girl was much less decisive and assured than her last rider, which worried her sometimes, but Molly appreciated her gentleness and compassion.

She'd helped the girl out at a fence earlier, despite feeling the lack of commitment and trust, and was rewarded with a glorious glow of gratitude from her. That, combined with the sudden appearance of a pony in front of her, had made her blood surge so much, she'd been unable to listen to her rider's instructions. The result of that had shocked and unsettled her, reminding her that taking matters into her own hooves was not always a good idea. And so, although she reacted instinctively to the whistle, she waited for Amber to direct her.

Their round was smooth, effortless and without a fault. As they cleared the final fence and cantered easily through the finish, the crowd roared. She heard whistles, whoops and wild applause. Still cantering around the arena, stroking Molly's mane lovingly, an array of smiling faces blurred together like melting wax as her eyes misted over. "Good lass," she spoke softly to her pony as they left the arena, applause still ringing in her ears. "I'm sorry I called you stupid. You're not stupid at all, you're brilliant. I'm the stupid one."

Amber let Jo have her jodhpurs back for the presentation as she wasn't placed so could put her tracky bottoms back on, but Jo had come fourth so couldn't go to the presentation in her pyjamas. First and second place went to members of Brantfort Pony Club. "Their ponies are used to this course. They practise on it all the time,"

Emily whispered cynically. Chelsea had come third. She'd jumped the alternative at the ditch and rails. Skylark had proved to be unreliable at the ditch here in the past so Chelsea had decided not to risk it. She'd picked up fifteen penalties, but her excellent dressage score helped her to stay ahead of Jo and Merry. They'd only had four jumping faults but their dressage hadn't been as good, dropping Jo into fourth. Finally, a girl and boy Amber had seen before but didn't know, from another club in the county, took fifth and sixth place and got the orange and purple rosettes. Several riders had been eliminated on the cross-country, meaning that Emily and Amber finished in seventh and eighth respectively, though there were no rosettes for them.

They waited for the final presentation of the Open class, but the new DC had an unexpected announcement to make.

"Erm, hem, hem," she began, "ladies and gentlemen, before we go on to the Open class results, there's an additional prize I'd like to present." Riders, mothers, fathers and helpers looked at each other in surprise, wondering what the additional prize would be.

"It isn't one we usually present… in fact, we've just made it up today, in the light of certain…er…events." She chuckled nervously as she turned and picked up a bunch of hastily bought petrol station flowers from the table of trophies and rosettes. "I apologise that it isn't something better but we didn't know we'd be doing this today." Pausing for effect, she looked around at the expectant faces, pleased to see they were hanging on her every word. Blushing slightly, she scanned the audience until her eyes settled on Amber.

"We'd like to present these to… Amber Anderson. Come on Amber!"

Amber spluttered like a fish and turned as pink as a cooked lobster. "Me? Wha…?" Her parents pushed her forward so that everyone could see her. Mrs Winnaker, the DC reached for her hand and pulled her into the middle of the presentation area. "Don't be shy Amber. These are for you." The flowers were handed to her and Mrs Winnaker put her arm around Amber. To everyone else, it looked like a warm embrace. Only the most observant would have seen Mrs Winnaker's grip tighten as she tried to prevent Amber from running away.

Amber felt like a butterfly pinned to a board, with all eyes on her, boring into her. She squirmed under Mrs Winnaker's grip and tried to slide back into the crowd, but Mrs Winnaker held on.

"Hang on, hang on! She's trying to run away!" She said, and the audience tittered. "I just want to say that…well, you've been an inspiration today. To remount and complete the course after taking a ducking in our swamp was impressive enough but to then go on and complete the event with a clear round show jumping…well, just remarkable. And we just wanted to say…well done!"

Amber wished she could teleport right out of there but when Mrs Winnaker released her to use both hands to join with the applause, she made do with sidling back towards her friends and family, grateful when everyone's attention returned to the prize-giving for the final class.

***

For a few days afterwards, Amber was stiff and sore. Considering she'd been wearing a body protector and had a soft landing, she couldn't understand where all the aches and pains came from. She also couldn't work out why she had a large mottled bruise all over her left forearm.

As well as the physical aches and pains, Amber's brain was worn out too as she see-sawed between the dizzying high of Molly's success at jumping, and the sinking low of the disastrous ending to the cross-country. She could accept that it was a mistake and was unlikely to happen again, but that didn't stop her from replaying the memory in her mind.

It bothered Amber that she'd only managed to ride well at the end, in the show jumping, because she knew she was no longer in the competition so her result didn't matter. *I really can't handle pressure*, she thought. She'd decided at Pony Club camp the previous summer that she wasn't interested in chasing trophies and rosettes – so long as she felt pleased with her own performance, she didn't care whether she won or not. She still felt like that, so couldn't work out why she got so nervous. *Is it the fear of falling off and getting hurt, or it all going wrong and making a fool of myself in front of everyone? Is it because I don't want to let Molly down and not be worthy of her?* Amber suspected all the reasons were valid, but with the local inter-branch tetrathlon not far away, she also knew she was terrified of letting the team down. In her sleep, she dreamed of making a series of catastrophic errors in every phase that meant she was by far the discount score. Amber was seriously considering telling her parents that she wanted to pull out.

They were acting very strangely too. Whenever she saw them, they gave her big grins and patted her on the head or shoulder like she was a dog or horse they were pleased with. She pouted, trying to work out whether they were genuine about being proud of her or...if they were trying too hard and pretending.

A ride out with Jo did nothing to allay her fears. Neither of them had attended Blakefield's Easter Monday gymkhana as both girls were giving their mounts a few days' rest, so Amber rode Pearl and Jo came out on her brother's pony, Sam. He hadn't competed yesterday as Matthew refused to learn a dressage test. Jo chattered away as usual, with Amber barely listening.

"Are you listening to me?" Jo asked.

"What Jo? Yes, sorry...?"

"I knew you weren't. I was just saying about calling me JoJo from now on."

"Er, what?" Amber realised she must have been somewhere else entirely. She had no idea what her friend was talking about.

"Well, everyone at school, even the teachers, have started calling me JoJo, 'cos I'm Joanne Jones. And it's cool, so I want you to call me JoJo too."

"Oh, right, yeah," Amber muttered. It was bad enough that Jo actually was cool, now she had a cool name as well. Her only nickname had been Amber Pamber which her parents had called her when she was young. She had banned them from using it when she started school as it was so cringey. If people started using her initials as a nickname, she'd be AA. She didn't know which was worse.

"What's wrong with you?" JoJo interrupted her thoughts. "You seem a bit down. You're not disappointed about the weekend, are you? Things can go wrong on the cross-country – that's what makes it so exciting. But your show jumping was fab. I couldn't believe it was you to be honest, when I think back to that first time in our paddock with Pearl. You'll be brill in the tetrathlon now that Molly has seen the course. You'll go clear for sure."

"Hmmm." Amber appreciated JoJo's encouraging words but wasn't convinced.

"Yeah, it's in the bag. You'll just need to practise opening gates and doing the slip rail so you don't pick up any penalties from those." JoJo kicked her feet out of the stirrups and let her legs dangle by Sam's side. They were so long now; her feet were level with his knees.

"What?" Amber was suddenly alert. "We have to open a gate? Why?" An image of the last time she'd tried to open a gate on Molly flashed before her eyes: her lying broken on the ground while the pony galloped off and left her there, alone.

"Yeah. Didn't you know?" JoJo's blue eyes were wide. "It's in the rulebook online." Amber shook her head. They'd been told about the rulebook but she hadn't got around to reading it yet. She'd assumed the adults would make sure they knew everything they needed to.

"On the cross-country, riders have to open a gate, mounted. You can't get off to do it. Well, you can, but I think you get two-hundred penalties. You've got to open it, go through and close it again within a minute or it's fifty penalties. And then somewhere else on the course, there'll be a slip rail. For that, you've got to get off, take down the top rail, get yourself and the pony over the bottom rail, put the top one back up and get back on. You've got one minute to get the top rail put back and remount. I'm sure that's right. And it's fifty penalties if you don't get it done in time."

Fear flared in Amber's mind like a peacock's tail at the mention of dismounting and remounting an excited pony that didn't want to stand around waiting for her rider.

"Can you have help? Can someone hold the pony for you?" *So it doesn't take-off while you're trying to get on*, she added to herself.

"Er...no." JoJo sensed Amber's apprehension. "If anyone helps you, you get penalties. Sixty, I think. But you'll be fine. You just need to practise. Maybe you should try learning to vault on like I do. It's way easier, especially as you'll have your stirrups shorter than usual on the cross-country." With that, she slipped off Sam's left side and as soon as her feet touched the ground, she bounced and leapt back on, almost going straight over the other side, as he was much smaller than Merry.

Amber knew the trick was designed to lighten the mood and make her smile, but it didn't work. She completed the ride in near silence, tuning JoJo out as she continued chattering about this and that. By the time they returned to the farm track and she dropped JoJo at her place, Amber realised with a sinking feeling that she had two choices: she could either ride Honey in the tetrathlon as she had always planned to, or she could drop out. That way she could either be replaced or the team could compete without her as a three. But riding Molly was no longer an option. The very idea of having to remount her in an open space where she could see other ponies whizzing around was out of the question. Look at what had just happened when Molly had seen another pony in front of her. Amber's hands trembled at the mere thought of it.

I'm back to square one, she thought miserably as she rode back into the farmyard on Pearl. The first sight that greeted her was Molly's beautiful face looking over her stable door, her white blaze flashing in the sun. A tear rolled down Amber's cheek as the revelation settled on her like a deadly snowstorm and chilled her to the bone.

Molly wasn't the pony for her.

She leaned forward and buried her face in Pearl's mane, the tears falling unchecked into the rough blackness. Pearl remained still, sensing her rider's anguish and feeling the sobs that wracked her body. *I'm still afraid of her*, Amber admitted to herself. I'm such a failure.

Oh, Pearl, what am I going to do?

As if she understood, Pearl snorted. It was like she was trying to answer, but whatever she might have been saying, Amber wasn't listening. The snakes in her stomach had returned, writhing, hissing and slithering up into her throat, choking her. Another sob escaped through her gritted teeth and Molly pricked her ears towards the sound. Through her cloudy eyes, Amber noticed how serene Molly looked, gazing over her door happily. But the warm wave of love that enveloped her was stabbed with a splinter of ice as the memory of lying painfully in the mud while the pony abandoned her jumped back into her mind. She was brilliant, beautiful and talented: all the traits anyone would want in a pony. But the most important thing, the thing she had with both of the Fell ponies, was missing, and without it there could be no future for them: trust.

She didn't trust Molly and without trust...end of story.

Author's Note

When I got Molly, aged thirteen, it was with competitions in mind. I wanted to compete with the riders I saw winning and have a chance against them. In Molly I saw a pony who could get me to where I wanted to be. What I didn't see was that I wasn't ready for her.

It's funny how you can learn lessons in life, but not apply them to other situations. From Pearl, I learned that ponies are all individuals, yet I didn't look for anything in Molly beyond her ability. From Honey I learned that pony and rider need to be a team, but I expected Molly to carry me to victory, despite the fact that I was still quite inexperienced. I wanted her to be the perfect pony. The problem is, there's no such thing.

Molly was as different to the Fell ponies I'd had before her as it was possible to be. We had a lot of problems and it affected my confidence. At the time, I felt that everything was her fault, but now looking back I can see that the problems were due to us being mismatched at the start of our relationship. If we had met several years later, when I had more experience of different ponies under my belt, things could have been a lot different.

I don't want to say too much more as Molly's story isn't over – it will continue in the fourth book – but I do wish I could apologise to her as I must have been a huge cause of frustration to her! Not that she was blameless – she did gallop off with me while I was mounting her and left me with a broken collarbone and she did go for a play on the bypass after somehow escaping from her field.

And, of course, she did dump me in the foulest water jump ever after trying to jump the whole thing. I got back on and finished but I didn't have someone to lend me a nice pair of dry jodhs. I completed my show jumping round that day covered in mud and slime. I thought if I wrote that in the book, readers would think it was too far-fetched, but sometimes the truth is stranger than fiction!

Acknowledgements

I'll start with huge thanks to all the readers and reviewers of the 'Amber's Pony Tales' books. Some have left reviews on Amazon, some have contacted me directly and some have done both! It's always amazing to hear from people of all ages who have enjoyed the books and I really appreciate the time people take to get in touch and share their comments. It means such a lot.

My appreciation also goes out to those who got involved with competitions and activities connected to the books. Marlyn and Isobel have found themselves with characters named after them in this book for entering the 'Little Pearl' writing competition, as have Maia and Elise for being beta readers and providing valuable pre-publication feedback on the unedited version of this story. To everyone who got involved with the cover star competition for this book: thank you. Hundreds of pictures were received but as the series' first two book covers (supplied by Let's Get Booked) are so incredible, the standard was very high so only the very best pictures were accepted. Many people who submitted photographs, but were not successful, still wished me luck in my search for the perfect pony to represent Molly and their positivity was beautiful. As was Strawberry, the eventual winner of the competition, who you can now see on the cover of this book. Big thanks to Myla Postlethwaite-Todd and her mum, Kate, for entering her.

For the cover of this book, I owe lots of Glenfiddich to Neil Routledge for his photography skills and I need to send a box of Galaxy bars over to Amanda Horan in Ireland for her services once again with cover design, editing and preparing this book in every way for publication.

To the teachers who've invited me in to schools to work with their students, I thank you for supporting me as an author and for promoting reading and writing to your students. I love working with children and some that I've met through author visits are definitely potential authors-in-the-making.

And finally, Katy for proof reading and Perrin for helping me to promote the books and reach more people. Thank you.

About the Author

Helen lives in Cumbria with her husband and horses, plus Bella the Dalmatian, Petra the crazy pointer and a variety of hens, ducks and geese.

Helen has been animal mad all her life. Her adventures with ponies began back in 1990 with Pearl and Honey, but they are still continuing now with her three horses, Maddy, Charlie and Holly who are all just as interesting and individual as Pearl and Honey were, and will probably end up in a book in the future too! Watch out for them.

Maddy is the old lady of the herd, and the cheeky one. She's full of personality and mischief. She's got herself into more trouble over the years than all the rest of the horses put together. She's semi-retired now, but still enjoys hacking out.

Then there's Charlie, the opinionated one, who thinks he's a thoroughbred racehorse but was sadly born into the body of a draft horse. He loves jumping, beach rides and charging about on cross-country courses.

Finally, there's Holly, who's a sensitive girl but with plenty of sass too!

When Helen isn't busy writing books or playing with horses, she can be found being a libress (something a student once called her – perhaps an appropriate title for a librarian who has been known to roar on occasion) and English teacher at a secondary school in the Lake District. She also writes books with children through her Writers & Illustrators club. They write as a team under the pseudonym K.S. Aitken.

For free bonus material linked to this book, plus news, competitions, and exclusive opportunities connected to the author's other books, sign up to the mailing list at www.helenharaldsen.co.uk

Did you enjoy this book? The author would love to see your reviews on Amazon. Please feel free to post your comments and let others know about Amber's Pony Tales.

Follow Amber's Pony Tales on Facebook.

Lightning Source UK Ltd.
Milton Keynes UK
UKHW010440161220
375272UK00002B/256

9 781916 011274